CHILDHOOD SWEETHEARTS IV

JACOB SPEARS

GOOD2GO PUBLISHING

Childhood Sweethearts IV
Written by Jacob Spears
Cover design: Davida Baldwin
Typesetter: Mychea
ISBN: 9781943686674

Copyright ©2016 Good2Go Publishing
Published 2016 by Good2Go Publishing
7311 W. Glass Lane • Laveen, AZ 85339
www.good2gopublishing.com
https://twitter.com/good2gobooks
G2G@good2gopublishing.com
www.facebook.com/good2gopublishing
www.instagram.com/good2gopublishing

Dedication

To my fans—a word of advice: One mistake could ruin our lives. So let's be wise when it comes to making decisions. God made it possible for us to learn from others' mistakes to better our lives. So let's learn and make wise decisions.

Also, to Satchel, the love of my life. My one and only. My true soul mate.

Acknowledgements

Lt. Bettineschi, Sgt. Joseph, sorry I called you old. What I meant was prehistoric. Ha-ha! Bettineschi told me about how you lived in a cave with a pet dinosaur. I'd like to acknowledge my mother, Lenora Sarantos, and my sisters Amy McKinney and Heather Hopkins. Also, I want to give a shout out to Landi, Quebman, Bad Nurse! Yeah! You know who you are! Bad, bad nurse! Novoa, thanks for getting me my time on the kiosk. And to you, Sgt. Glass.

Most important, to Trayvon D. Jackson. Without him, this book wouldn't be possible.

1

Stone couldn't believe his eyes when he pulled up on Smooth. It was evident from the bullet holes and shattered windows of his car that nothing alive was inside. A small crowd began to gather and became bystanders of the scene. Stone though fast.

"I gotta get my shit!" Stone said to himself.

He parked directly behind Smooth's truck, hopped out with a ski mask over his face, and raided the backseat of Smooth's truck as the crowd looked on. Stone grabbed the drugs and Smooth's AK-47 lying on the backseat. He took a look at Smooth hunched over in the front seat and badly wanted to catch the ones who had just killed his connect.

"If I ever catch 'em, man, me got you!" Stone said to Smooth before quickly leaving the scene before the police showed.

He had to dump the stash car and kill anything connected to the tag—his clientele.

* * *

Two days later

"Homie, I still don't see nothing 'bout the negro!" Mario said to his M-13 Mexican brother and superior, Juan, who was watching television for news updates.

"Maybe the police don't want to expose him, homie," Juan responded back to Mario, who was sitting on the sofa eating a spicy burrito and drinking Mexican rum on ice.

Juan José was the leader of the lethal M-13s in Miami, who were rivals of the M-14s and Smooth's spreading organization. Juan had been the top cocaine distributor until Smooth's business began crippling his money. He wanted Smooth dead and had finally caught him slipping at the gas station. It was music to his ears when he got the call from his lieutenant, Pascal, that Smooth was dead.

"Now we will lay back and see who is bold enough to step into his shoes!" Juan said before he dropped to the floor to do push-ups.

He was a short, cocky Mexican man at five five and 150 pounds, who resembled Joker from *Next Friday*. He could have a man and his family killed at the snap of his fingers.

On the other hand, Mario stood five six, weighed 165 pounds, and was the right-hand man to Juan. He too had mad respect in the streets, and he loved murder like a fat kid loves Coke.

"We lost two yesterday. Do you think that was them or our rivals?" Mario asked, wiping his mouth with a napkin before sucking on the straw from a cup of iced rum.

"Who knows? It could have been anyone!" Juan said before breathlessly standing up for a break. "If it was them Negros, then we're still strong, minus two, as opposed to their head man.'"

* * *

When Smooth awoke at Jackson Memorial Hospital, he was deeply perplexed as to where the hell he was. Last he remembered, he was on his death bed after being caught slipping. A nurse saw his eyes open, and spoke.

"Welcome, Smooth. I'm Nurse Tara, and I'm taking your vitals right now. I'm a friend of Spencer's," she said with a smile.

"Karen! He's awake!" Nurse Tara screamed for her partner.

"Is he really?" Nurse Karen said as she came running into the room.

She stood at the end of the bed with her hands on her hips.

"Am I alive?" Smooth asked in a harsh voice from an extremely dry sore throat.

"Yes! You are alive, baby!" Smooth heard China's voice from the side of him.

When Smooth looked over, he saw the gorgeous China smiling at him while wiping away unbridled tears cascading down her face.

"China!" Smooth smiled, clearing this throat.

"Yes, babe! It's me. No dream. All real, too," China said as she stood and modeled for Smooth, spinning around in a circle.

Since her release, she had been by Smooth's side, supporting him through both of his operations. Smooth had lost most of his left ear and was shot in his shoulder and left thigh. The Kevlar vest had saved his life once again. Smooth was glad to see his baby, China, back on the streets with him. She definitely had grown, and looked like a voluptuous supermodel.

"Okay, your vitals are wonderful. But, um, how do I tell you this? But I have to. You've lost most of your ear."

"Ear!" Smooth shouted, feeling for his ear with his free arm. However, he was unable to determine which ear he had lost because of the bandage wrapped around his head. In fact, both ears were in pain. "What do you mean?"

"Smooth, an ear loss is better than your damn life being taking any day!" China said, trying to comfort him.

She didn't care if he lost both arms and legs as long as his heart could beat.

"You were also shot in your left shoulder, which explains the sling, Smooth," Nurse Tara went on to explain about his condition. "Another bullet that came through the driver's door pierced through your thigh. It was retrieved, and the bleeding has stopped," Tara continued.

"Look at it this way. You're still alive!" Nurse Karen added.

"I'm hungry and very thirsty. When will I be able to leave?" Smooth asked both nurses.

Tara looked at Karen for a response, since she was Smooth's lead nurse.

"Well, how about we let you stay one more night until you try to go home, so we can release you with medication."

"No! I need to get out of here today!" Smooth snapped.

"Really!" China exclaimed.

"Let them treat you, Smooth. I've been here by your side, and I'm not going nowhere. There's nothing to be in a rush for out there in the world. I'm home now!" China checked Smooth.

* * *

Sue Rabbit was in the trap house making sure everything stayed under control. The product was getting low, and it was driving Sue Rabbit nuts, as he was praying and hoping that he didn't run out of product before Smooth was released from the hospital. He was sitting on the sofa watching the Packers play the Cowboys, when Prince Guru's car system rattled the apartment windows.

"Damn! That nigga's shit beatin' hard!" Sue Rabbit said as he stood and walked over to unlock the door for Guru.

Less than a minute later, Guru walked through the door with a black Adidas duffel bag, which he handed over to Sue Rabbit.

"This is all the money from 112th," Prince Guru said. "All we waiting on now is the Pokabean Projects to come through."

"Good, man! We about to run low on product, and that'll fuck up business. If I can't get a brick from you, then I'ma go to the next man. Feel me?" Sue Rabbit said to Prince Guru, who clearly understood what he was inferring.

"What's on yo' mind, nigga?" Prince Guru asked, with a smile on his face.

"Shit! You already know what's on my mind!" Sue Rabbit retorted.

"Say no more, nigga. We moving tonight," Prince Guru said.

2

" M e speak no English! Me no English!" the Mexican screamed in devastating pain from Spencer's torturing.

Spencer had been out snatching up Mexicans and trying to find the shooters who tried to kill Smooth. The Mexican man was dangling from a rope tied to a joist in an abandoned building that Spencer had purchased for one purpose: to slaughter his victims.

Pssst!

"Awww! No English!" the man shouted after being shot with a BB.

"Who's your boss, my friend?" Spencer asked for the umpteenth time, yet still getting the same results.

"My amigo! You're making me mad!" Spencer said as he walked in circles around the man while pumping his BB gun for another intense round.

"So, I see we're going to do this, amigo!" Spencer continued, stopping in front of his victim.

He crossed his arms and scratched his head.

"You're going to die!"

"No! No! No!" the man cried.

"Ah! So you do comprende!" Spencer replied with an evil smirk on his face.

He aimed the BB gun at the Mexican's left eyeball.

"My sharpshooting days pay off now!" Spencer said as he pulled the trigger and nailed the man in the right eyeball.

"Awwww!" he shrilled in more devastating pain.

"Yeah! I know it's a bitch, huh?" Spencer said over the Mexican's cries.

Spencer then pumped the BB gun for another intense round and shot him through his mouth.

Pssst!

Spencer shook the BB gun and saw that it was empty.

"Fuck! Shit! Ass! Fuck!" Spencer exploded.

He then tossed the gun to the ground and removed his Glock .21 from the waist of his jeans.

"Since you don't know, then I don't know," Spencer said as he released the whole clip into the man, who unbeknownst to him was Juan José's uncle.

* * *

It didn't take nightfall long to catch Sue Rabbit and Prince Guru. They were back to their routine down in Martin County, before coming to work for Smooth.

"Back to robbing 'migos!" Sue Rabbit said to Guru while sitting in the passenger seat of the stolen Dodge Caravan.

"The only thing about these niggas is that they know where that cake at," Guru said to Sue.

"Well, let's go!" Sue Rabbit said as he pulled down his ski mask and hopped out of the van carrying his MAC-10.

They ran inside a store on 189th where the Mexicans sold drugs from behind the counter. It was a come-up that Guru had been contemplating for a rainy day like today.

"Get the fuck down on the ground!" Sue Rabbit screamed as he came through the door, shooting two clerks off the jump, leaving only one man standing.

"Where's the coke at, amigo?" Sue Rabbit asked the store clerk. "Lie to me, and I'll turn your head into a tomato!" Sue Rabbit continued as Guru rushed into the back office and began rummaging through the desk and drawers.

"Thee money in safe!"

"Fuck yo' money! Where is the dope?" Sue Rabbit demanded.

"Okay! Okay! I show you the coke," the clerk said with his hands raised in the air.

Sue Rabbit rushed behind the counter and grabbed the Mexican man by his long ponytail. An old lady tried to enter the store, and Sue shot her between her eyes.

"Let's go, or you'll be next!" Sue Rabbit explained to the shaking man, who was now afraid for his life.

"Bingo!" Sue heard Guru scream before he made it back to the office himself.

When he entered the office, he saw Guru standing on a chair and pulling down a box from a removed panel in the ceiling. Inside the box was one hundred kilos of cocaine.

Boom!

Sue Rabbit shot the Mexican man in the head, and then he helped Guru pull down another box.

* * *

China was bathing Smooth in the bathroom in his hospital room. She washed him thoroughly, making sure he was clean.

"I still don't see why we couldn't go home today," he said.

China sucked her teeth and rolled her eyes. She was tired of repeatedly hearing Smooth bitch about going home.

"Smooth, I promise if you say that shit again, we gonna have some problems. I'm bathing you, going home to grab some pajamas and feed Zorro. That makes two of us. If I can do it, then you can too. What's another day?" she questioned.

China didn't understand the responsibility that Smooth now had since her incarceration. He had men who needed him and clientele to keep happy in order to keep a dollar in his pockets. Smooth was moving in the big league, and he had competition against him that obviously wanted him dead.

Smooth ignored China's adamant decision to keep him in the hospital. He knew she was only looking out for him. When China took the sponge and cleaned his dick and balls, he couldn't resist an erection. China smiled and gave him a naughty look.

"Don't look at me like that!" Smooth said, biting down on his bottom lip and licking his lips. "How much you miss me?" he asked.

"More than you," China said in a sexy manner while stroking Smooth slowly yet effectively. "This is messed up,

Smooth. Why'd you have to go and get yourself shot?"
China asked, still stroking his dick.

"Because your nigga's the man in Miami now, and these
Mexicans want me to lay down!"

"What are you going to do, Smooth? We don't need the
dope life no more. I'm home now. I can't lose you to these
Latin-ass Mexicans, baby. I know you have muthafuckas out
who'll kill for you. If they'll do that, then they'll work for
you!" China explained.

"I know, baby, but I can't leave my niggas on the front
line. While you were gone, these niggas not only helped me
rise, they held me down, boo!" he said to China.

"So you're gonna continue to be in the streets?" China
asked, and abruptly stopped stroking Smooth's dick.

She stared into his eyes with a mean mug like she was
ready to slap the shit out of him.

"Listen, baby. Even if I were to back out of the game, I
just can't walk away from an empire that I've built," Smooth
explained.

"No! But you could limit yourself from being in the
opening!" China exploded. "You know what? Come! Let's
get you dressed for bed, Smooth, because I'm two seconds
away from slapping the shit out of your dumb ass. Why do
you have to be so adamant and selfish?"

"How am I being selfish?" Smooth shouted. "China, I
have real niggas—not ducks—on my team," Smooth added.

"Fuck your team! How 'bout I go kill every last one of
them for being before me?" China questioned as she coldly
stormed from the bathroom, leaving Smooth in the tub.

"China, where are you going? Come here!" Smooth called out to her.

All he heard was the door slam.

Smooth knew that he had come off wrong by having too much love for his niggas compared to China. It didn't take him long to see things from her perspective. She wanted him to leave the game alone and leave his niggas the goldmine.

"I can't!" Smooth said to himself.

Prison really changed her, because the old China would teach me how to make a dollar, Smooth thought as he pressed the call button for a nurse assistant.

Nurses Tara and Karen were retired for the day. When Smooth saw the gorgeous blonde nurse come into his room, he couldn't help an erection.

"Need help out of there, Johnson?" she asked.

"Hell yeah!" Smooth retorted with an impish smile.

* * *

China was highly upset by Smooth's decision to continue to be a damn target. She wiped away tears as she drove over to Roxy's restaurant. She needed something to put in her stomach and get her mind off Smooth's stubbornness. When she pulled up, she saw that business was booming.

"Yes, may I help you?" the employee asked, with a sexy voice.

She was a beautiful redbone bitch with star tattoos behind her ears. China was awestruck at her beautiful cat eyes.

"Um, yeah. Tell Roxy that her sister is out here, um," China said, looking at the girl's name tag on her shirt, "Tracy."

"Okay. Well, we have a special table reserved for you. It's the table in the back," Tracy pointed, but China wasn't looking at any table.

She was mesmerized by Tracy. When Tracy turned her head back and saw China gawking, she blushed.

"Are you bi?" Tracy asked.

"Are you down?" China asked.

"You're serious!" Tracy asked.

"What time do you get off?" China asked.

"In five minutes."

"How 'bout you forget telling my sister I came. I'll be waiting on you to come out to the parking lot. We're going to my place. Do you mind?" China asked.

"No, I'm down," Tracy said as she walked off with a sexy-ass pep in her step.

She has ass, too, China thought.

* * *

Banga pulled up to the trap house and saw Sue Rabbit's and Guru's cars outside. He was bringing them re-up money and owed cash to Smooth. Banga was frustrated. He had no more product, and he wasn't sure if Sue and Guru had any.

"What's up, Sue Rabbit and Guru?" Banga said, dapping them both when he came inside the trap house.

It was just Sue Rabbit and Guru. Banga didn't notice any workers. He then handed over the duffel bag that he had brought inside with him.

"Two things, two problems," Banga started.

Sue grabbed the bags and carried them to the kitchen.

"What's on your mind, Banga?" Sue Rabbit asked.

"No product and no Smooth. No one knows when he'll get out of the hospital," Banga said, shaking his head in frustration.

"Well, our only problem is we need someone to cook. Other than that, we have plenty of product. We don't know who Smooth had cooking up his shit!" Sue Rabbit said, sparking flame to a blunt.

"Shit! All these fiends. I'm sure all of them know how to cook," Banga said.

"Yo! I ain't trusting no fiend, even if I'm watching him cook the shit in front of me!" Sue Rabbit said.

"Then how 'bout we all watch 'im cook it, and then kill his ass when we're done with him," Banga suggested.

"Now that we could do! At least I can get over the feeling of being robbed by a fiend. Them muthafuckas would rob you blind butt naked!" Sue Rabbit replied.

"Well, let's get this shit rolling," Guru said, clapping his hands, ready to get started.

3

China didn't waste any time ripping off Tracy's clothes when they stepped through the front door. Before China brought Tracy into her room, she locked Zorro inside the guest room. She then laid Tracy down on the sofa and kissed her on her sexy lips.

"Ummm!" Tracy moaned.

While kissing her, China rapidly finger-fucked her pussy, inserting an additional finger every couple of strokes.

"Uhhh, shit!" Tracy moaned out when China inserted all four fingers.

China moved down and began sucking on Tracy's clitoris.

"Damn! This pussy is pretty!" China complimented her while still finger-fucking her.

"Thank you!" Tracy purred loudly.

China cuffed her thumb and balled her hand into a fist and got her hand inside Tracy's expanding pussy.

Wow! China thought as she rammed her fist into Tracy's extremely wet pussy.

"Lord! Ummmm! I'm coming!" Tracy shouted out, convulsing and panting.

China pulled out her fist and made Tracy lick it clean.

"Mmmmm!" Tracy exclaimed, tasting her juices.

"Are you satisfied?" China asked.

"Yes, I am. Can I return the favor now?" Tracy asked.

China looked at her watch and saw that she couldn't spare the time. She had to be back at the hospital with Smooth before visitation hours were over or they wouldn't let her back to his room.

"Sorry, but I have to get going. Maybe we could link up again."

"Most definitely, and next time, I'm going first with my toys!" Tracy promised as she kissed China and then put her clothes back on.

China walked Tracy to the door and kissed her once more. When Tracy was gone, China released Zorro, who came running up to her and stood on his back legs, happy to see her.

"I miss you too, baby," China said to Zorro, who began licking the hand with which she had just fucked Tracy.

"She taste good, huh, boy?" China asked Zorro.

China fed the dog, took a quick shower, and then grabbed her pajamas. She then noticed that the time was 8:45 and visitation ended at 9:00 p.m.

"Let me get out of here," China said as she dashed out the front door.

* * *

When China walked into the room, she saw the pretty blonde fluffing out Smooth's pillow and being a little bit too damn friendly. China cleared her throat and made her presence known.

"Oh, you must be China. He's been telling me a lot about you!" the blonde nurse exclaimed.

"Yes, I am. Is he taken care of?" China asked.

"Of course he is. I'll leave you two alone to yourself. Ummm," she said, looking at her Mickey Mouse watch, "I'll be back at 9:45 p.m. to take his vitals, and then it's just you two again until 3:00 a.m. Okay?" Sandy the nurse said.

"Okay, thanks for your help," China said politely while giving Smooth a nasty look.

"You're welcome," Sandy said before strutting out of the room.

China walked to the door with Sandy and closed it behind her. She then turned around with her hands on her hips, with an impish grin on her face.

"What's that look for?" Smooth asked as China walked to the bed, snatched back the covers, and noticed Smooth's bulge through his hospital gown.

China lifted his gown and grabbed his dick.

"Was it me or her?" China asked. "And be honest!"

"What kind of question is that?" he asked as he leaned forward to kiss China.

When his lips touched hers, her entire body was rocked with an electrifying wave of ecstasy. She let out a soft moan that caused Smooth's dick to throb even more. Smooth pulled her closer and kissed her on her neck.

"That's my spot!" China panted.

"Daddy remembers," Smooth said as he tugged on China's pajama shirt and let her breasts spill out.

He caressed her right breast and then sucked on her erect nipple.

"What you miss about me?" China asked in a purr.

"Everything, baby! Come out of everything and give me what belongs to me!" Smooth demanded.

"Yes, daddy," China purred as she disrobed and climbed into bed with Smooth, being careful not to hurt him.

She reversed and squatted down on his dick, and slowly made passionate love to him. Smooth's mind was blown when he saw how artistic she was now when making love to him.

4

Stone didn't hear anything on the local news about the death of Smooth, which made him think that Smooth was just another forgotten, irrelevant statistic. He was extremely upset because Smooth was a good connect. Smooth was his lifeline, and now he had no decent connect to cop from. Like he'd promised Smooth, Stone gathered a couple of his goons and traveled from Little Haiti to Chico Town in Miami. On the way, he passed a crime scene where they were bringing out bodies from inside a corner store.

"Someone done flip the Mexican, Ramen!" Stone said to his head goon driving the SUV.

In the backseat were two of his sergeants, Jamaican Joe and Rosco, who were born to kill and only lived to kill.

"Turn on 123rd, man. We hitting the trap house," Stone directed Ramen.

When Ramen turned down the street, a group of Mexicans was partying at a white rooming house, just as Stone knew they would be on a Friday night. It was one of Juan's brothels and a place to come do drugs. Ramen slowly drove past the house to peep the scene.

"Go to the end and turn around," Stone said to Ramen, who did as he was instructed.

When they came back on the scene, Ramen halted two houses down. Stone and the duo in the backseat hopped out with AK-47s and rushed the brothel while simultaneously releasing AK-47 rounds and hitting everything in sight. Stone and his men then ran inside when they'd hit everyone outside, and did a number on everyone indoors as well.

"Muthafuckas, you mess with me money, man!" Stone screamed as he continued to add to the death toll.

Satisfied with their work, Stone and his goons made a successful getaway, leaving behind fifty dead Mexicans who were only out to have a good time.

* * *

"Hey, homie, the brothel just got hit!" Mario shook Juan, waking him from his sleep on the sofa.

Juan awoke deeply confused from an almost wet dream. He hadn't heard Mario clearly, so he asked him to repeat what he had just said. "What the fuck, homes?"

"Man, somebody just hit the brothel. Fifty are dead!"

"What? Are you serious?" Juan said in complete shock.

"These Negros not playing, homie!" Mario expressed.

Earlier, Juan's uncle was robbed and then killed at the corner store, and now Juan's brothel, which was one of his big money spots, was hit. Despite knowing that Mario was serious, Juan still had to go see with his own eyes.

"Come, homes!" Juan said as he grabbed his MAC-11 and stormed out the front door.

He hopped inside his black lowrider Ford F150 truck and drove over to 123rd, where he was met with a serious crime scene.

"Muthafucka!" Juan screamed before he slammed his hand on the steering wheel.

"Call Pascal and tell him to get everybody together. This shit is not going to fly over our heads, homie!" Juan said to Mario, who was already on the phone informing Pascal about what the boss was ordering.

* * *

"God damn! Look at this shit!" Sue Rabbit said to Guru and Banga, who were watching the fiend named Jeffery cook up the coke.

Sue had the television in the living room blasting on Channel 7 News.

"Breaking news here in Miami on 123rd, also known as Chico Town. A mass killing has taken place at the brothel behind me. Sadly, fifty people were killed. Metro-Dade police are investigating this and now are considering it to be a hit on M-13 gang affiliates. If you have any knowledge of the killers or people involved, please call our hotline at 800-447-8621. This is the second homicide in Chico Town today. Please! I'm Rachel Lopez reporting live for Channel 7 News," the reporter stated.

"Damn! Looks like somebody was really upset with the M-13s."

"Fuck 'em. We see they getting it, too. They tried taking our nigga out, so we take them. We got lil niggas ready to catch any of them creeping this way," Sue Rabbit said.

Sue was paying some goons to keep an eye out for any Mexicans coming through. He knew how vulnerable they looked without Smooth, especially since folks thought he was dead.

"Just continue to stay on point. Yo! I need fifty of them things, Jeffery, so I can hit up my clientele. So put some speed to that whip game you got," Banga said to the fiend who was converting coke in a pot into a rock substance.

"You've been saying that shit all night. Like I said, hurry up!"

Tat! Tat! Tat! Tat! Tat!

Everyone heard the nearby shots and then looked at each other without moving.

"That's a choppa!"

"No, a TEC-9, nephew!" Jeffery corrected Banga.

The shots continued, and everyone could hear the distinctive shots of exchanging gunfire.

Chop! Chop! Chop!

"Now that's a choppa, nephew," Jeffery said while whipping fast.

"Watch him," Sue said as he grabbed his AK-47 off the sofa and then stormed out the front door.

When Sue Rabbit saw the Chevy Impala with the Mexicans hanging out the window, he aimed at the Impala's back end and squeezed while his lil niggas held down the block with their AK-47s.

Chop! Chop! Chop! Chop!

Sue Rabbit surprised the Mexicans in the car and caused them to step on the gas and flee from the entrapment.

Damn! Something quieter would have knocked buddy's ass out! Sue Rabbit said to himself.

With the threat gone, niggas came from behind their shields with their hot AK-47s.

Whoever it was realized quickly that they had come down the wrong block to start a gun fight, Sue Rabbit thought as one of his goons named Mall walked up to him with his AK-47 strapped across his chest.

"I guess they think we slipping at three o'clock in the morning!" Mall said.

Sue Rabbit raised his hand in the air and got a high five from Mall, who was a ruthless eighteen-year-old who had dropped out his first year in high school. He was swarthy looking, stood five eight, and weighed 186 pounds. Without his teeth, no one would see him. And that's exactly how he had tricked the Mexicans.

"Good job, my nigga!" Sue Rabbit said.

Boom!

Sue Rabbit heard a shot go off in the apartment. He quickly went to investigate, when he stepped inside and saw Banga in the kitchen with his Glock .40 in hand and no Jeffery. He knew half of what was going on. When he walked into the kitchen, he found Jeffery on the floor in front of the stove with a pool of blood beneath his head. He was dead.

"What? You thought he was gonna live? I bet the nigga socks full of dope, and we watched, too," Banga said, getting a smile from Sue Rabbit and a chuckle out of Guru.

Sue Rabbit pulled out his iPhone and called his clean-up crew, who would come and dispose of Jeffery's body.

"Hello!"

"Get over here. I got a job for y'all!" Sue said into his phone before hanging up. "I guess this means he's done with everything?" Sue asked.

"Everything on time," Banga said.

5

Two months later

*I*t was quite a shocker when everyone learned that Smooth wasn't dead as many of his enemies and Stone had thought. For two months, Smooth had been letting Sue Rabbit run things while he moved around very little during his recovery. He was always home and making love to China when she was home from work. She had gotten herself a job at Roxy's and brought him home something delicious every night. Despite her unwillingness, she would always drive to New York with Smooth to see Jefe. For China's loyalty, Jefe bought her a new candy-apple-red Mercedes McLaren.

Looking at himself in the mirror, Smooth was ready to step back into the city with his niggas. He adjusted the Chicago Bulls cap on his head and pulled it over his ears. He still had to get used to missing an ear.

"It's time to go get this money," Smooth said as he inserted a round in both of his Glock .40s.

Sue Rabbit and Guru were sending niggas out on every corner to kill M-13 Mexicans. A Mexican with a blue bandana meant "kill on sight" to Smooth, and that's exactly what he and his men were doing. Thanks to Spencer, Smooth had learned of Juan José, the leader of the M-13s. Their beef was known, and Smooth was ready to catch Juan and Mario slipping. But they were smart and knew the art of war, unlike Smooth, who was making yet another mistake by stepping back on the front line instead of letting his soldiers hold him down.

"Zorro, come!" Smooth called out before grabbing his leash to take him for a walk.

When Zorro came to him, Smooth snapped his leash to his collar and then proceeded out the door.

* * *

China was working her ass off at Roxy's with her friends Jane and Tabby, who she had promised to set up with apartments and a job. She had even set them up on their first dates—one-night stands.

Tracy and China were still seeing each other and growing closer, something that Smooth was unaware of. China had no clue why she couldn't tell him about her girlfriend yet. It had been two months, and it was eating at her conscience that she was hiding something from him.

"I gotta tell him soon. I can't keep holding back from him, Tracy," China said, after eating her pussy in the parking lot during lunch break.

"Well, just tell him. How do you think he'll react?" Tracy asked.

"His birthday is coming up in two weeks. How about we give him a nice birthday present?" China questioned.

"A threesome?"

"Yeah, just us three," China said.

"Can I ask you a question for a truthful answer?"

"Yeah! Go ahead!" China answered.

"Do he has a big dick?"

"Does me eating that phat-ass pussy of yours feel good to you?" China answered a question with a question, giving Tracy her answer as well.

"I have another question."

"What's that?" China inquired.

"Would you let him fuck me in my ass while you fuck me with a dildo?"

China chuckled and almost pissed herself. She loved how Tracy was so blunt and an impudent freak.

"Girl, you're too much!"

"Come on! Answer the question!" Tracy purred as she slid over to China and kissed her softly.

They were in Tracy's big-body SUV behind tinted windows and loved to have quickies on their lunch breaks. Tracy's head was gone over China, and China loved her back.

"Yeah, we will accommodate all your freaky needs, okay?" China laughed.

"Look! There's your sister. She's looking for us." Tracy pointed out Roxy, who was standing at the front door with her hands on her hips and staring daggers at Tracy's truck.

"Let's go, because I don't want to hear her mouth," China said as she opened the door to step out.

When Roxy saw China step out, she walked back inside, seeing that she had made her point very clear.

* * *

When Amanda heard knocking at her front door, she quickly put on her robe to cover herself, and walked over to the door. When she opened it, she was happy to see Smooth standing in her doorway with a duffel bag.

"Hey, handsome. You chilling or dropping off?" she asked.

Since China had come home and he had been stopping by, Amanda and Smooth hadn't dealt with each other sexually, and it bothered Amanda because she wanted to feel him inside her. Smooth could see the loss in her eyes. But he didn't want to cheat on China.

It isn't like she isn't home. Her being in prison was another thing, but she isn't now, Smooth thought.

Smooth's silence of contemplation spoke loudly to Amanda.

"It's because of China, huh?" she asked.

"You already know, Amanda."

"You could have at least given me a warning that we were done. I would have made the last time like never before. Come in, Smooth. Leave everything on the counter. I have to put on some clothes," Amanda explained as she turned around.

Smooth followed her, stepped inside, and closed the door behind him.

"Come here, 'Manda," Smooth called out.

Amanda stopped and turned around, with tears in her eyes.

27

"What, Smooth?" she said, wiping away the tears.

She didn't want to tell him how much she had cried for him and had feelings for him, but there was no better time than now.

"Smooth, I thought you were dead. It was everywhere in the streets. I cried. Smooth, I'm not supposed to feel like this. But when you're the only one fucking me, it's inevitable, Smooth!" Amanda cried. "I can't tell you that there are no feelings, but for you to just walk around like I'm just your cook girl. Well, how do you think that makes me feel? Don't get me wrong! I'm not asking you to leave China or continue to fuck me. I can respect you being faithful, but damn, you could have fucked me good one last time."

Before Amanda could get one more word out, Smooth grabbed her in his arms and kissed her deeply. He then backed her up to the kitchen table and let her robe fall to the floor so he could caress her body. Amanda unfastened his belt and then let his pants fall to the floor, after removing his two Glock .40s. She climbed on the table, turned on her back, and sucked his dick backward while playing with her clitoris. As Amanda sucked Smooth's dick, she looked up at him as he stared into her eyes.

"Damn, ma!" he purred.

"Last time. We're going out with a bang!" Amanda promised.

"Oh yeah?" Smooth said as he felt himself about to come to his climax.

"I feel you coming, baby, please," Amanda purred as she stroked and sucked his dick until he exploded down her gullet.

"Damn!" Smooth shouted in ecstasy.

"This is only the beginning. Come to the room," she said as she led Smooth to the bedroom where they had hardcore sex like never before.

* * *

Sue Rabbit and Guru pulled up to the gym on 112th to work out. They had been coming to the gym for two weeks, lifting weights and hitting the pull-up bar. When they walked in, all the regulars were there, like the previous Fridays.

"Welcome again, you two," the manager, Mr. Body said.

Mr. Body was a muscle-bound black man in his late forties and in wonderful shape.

"We're always on time, Mr. Body," Sue Rabbit said as he and Guru handed him their membership cards to swipe.

When Sue looked at the workout pad, he caught the eye of a new member. She was busy doing squats and had a nice firm ass.

"Damn!" Sue Rabbit exclaimed, just as Guru looked over and became just as mesmerized.

"Who's that, Mr. Body?" Sue Rabbit asked.

"Oh her?" Mr. Body said as he stepped around the counter. "She's a season member."

"So she's been coming here?" Guru asked while making eye contact with the beautiful woman.

She stood five six and weighed 135 pounds, and she looked like she was an Italian or mixed chick.

"Looks like she needs a workout partner, Guru," Sue Rabbit said.

"Yeah! I'ma go see if I can give her a hand," Guru said as he strutted off toward the woman while Sue Rabbit went to push a couple reps on the bench press.

As Guru approached, the woman was doing a set of pull-ups. As she began to struggle, Guru grabbed her by her slim waist and helped her for another ten.

"Thanks!" she said breathlessly, after coming down from the bar.

"You're welcome."

"Landi!" She offered her hand and name to Guru, who took her delicate hand in his and shook it slowly while looking into her adorable brown eyes.

"Guru. Prince Guru, I mean."

"Guru as in an expert and person of wisdom?" Landi asked, with her hands planted on her hips. The sweat trickling down her flawless tanned skin made her look even sexier.

"Yeah, you got it right," Guru said proudly.

"So, I never seen you around here. Are you from Miami?" Landi asked, bending over to grab a pair of dumbbells and then beginning her reps.

"I'm from Martin County, but I've been down here for a few years now," Guru said.

"Do you like Miami?"

"Do I? I've fallen in love with this place. I barely go visit home," Guru explained.

"Who's the guy you came with? Your brother?"

Damn, this bitch is asking too many questions! Guru thought.

"That's my dawg Sue Rabbit."

"Sue Rabbit? What kind of name is that?" Landi asked.

"A family name passed down to him from his father."

"So tell me, Landi, what is your native that has me so confused?"

"If you had to guess, what would you say?" she questioned, dropping the dumbbells and then beginning to roll both arms forward.

"It's hard to tell, so forgive me if I'm wrong, but I'd say you're Italian."

"What are you, a womanizer, Mr. Guru a.k.a. expert?" Landi said with a smile.

"Damn! I must have struck gold, huh?" Guru said, impressed with himself for hitting it on the head.

"Silver," Landi said as she burst out laughing.

It was evident to them both that they were digging each other's personality and that there was an attraction. Suddenly, Landi cupped her smile in her hands and began to blush.

"So, what do you do for a living?" Guru asked curiously.

Landi dropped her arms and planted them back on her hips.

"I'm a sniper for the Metro-Dade SWAT unit," Landi replied.

Guru became speechless, not knowing if she was serious or not. So he asked Landi, who now had a smirk on her face, "You're serious?"

"No, silly, I'm only a guard at the Metro-Dade jail," Landi replied. "So, what is it that you do for a living?"

"I guess I'm the bad guy," Guru said honestly.

"I love the bad guys."

"Why?" Guru asked.

"Because they're brave and overprotective," she said, shooting Guru a curveball of her unfulfillment.

"In what aspect?"

"Relationships," Landi answered.

"May I ask?"

"No!" Landi joked.

"Are you single?"

"No, I'm not single. I just told you that I work for Metro-Dade. Last I checked, we were a gang," Landi said.

"Good one!"

"No, I'm not with anyone at the moment. Too much work and not enough time for relationships or friendships. At least that's what my ex tells me," Landi admitted as she grabbed her towel, wiped her face and arms, and then grabbed her water bottle. "What's your status, handsome?" she asked as she took a sip of water.

"I'm a free agent as of now, I guess," Guru replied.

"Do you like Italian food?"

"I'll eat any type of food, and if it's—" Guru paused "—never mind!"

"Maybe we could hook up some time and have dinner. I know this nice Italian restaurant on South Beach. I want to repay you for helping me out," she said.

"All I did was spot you on a couple pull-ups."

"That's a lot," Landi admitted.

"Fine," Guru said.

For the next five minutes, Landi and Guru exchanged phone numbers and chatted about different types of workouts. Sue Rabbit was getting his swole on while Guru got his mack on with Landi.

"You got ya one there," Sue Rabbit said to himself while watching Guru brighten up Landi's day.

Sue Rabbit's iPhone chimed, with Drake's new hit "Free" as the ring tone. He saw that it was Cherry.

"Hello," Sue Rabbit answered.

"Where are you?"

"I'm at the gym. What's up?"

"I miss you. Come scoop me."

"Give me an hour."

"Okay, I'll be waiting."

* * *

Jenny walked out of her cell in a hurry when she heard her name for mail pickup being called. She and her new cellmate, Amber, were playing spades, and Jenny was winning most of the games.

"Jenny Davis! Jenny Davis! Jenny Davis!" the guard continued to call out, dropping letter after letter on the day room table.

"That gotta be China. That girl ain't never get no mail," an inmate said behind Jenny.

"Bitch! Whoever you are, I don't need y'all in my business," Jenny snapped.

"Young lady, watch your conduct!" the guard said to Jenny, who grabbed all her mail and walked away.

"Jenny Davis! More mail!" the guard called back out just as Jenny got to her cell.

She turned around and went back to receive her last piece of mail. It was a JPay receipt. When Jenny looked at the amount, her eyes began to water. China had sent $5,000 to her inmate account, along with cards, letters, and pictures.

Thank you so much! Jenny thought.

She read every letter and couldn't stop looking at the pictures. She avoided resuming playing cards with her cellmate and started immediately responding back to China's letters.

Dear China,

Girl—you are amazing. What would I do without you? Thank you for the pictures and letters, plus the money. Come see me like you promised. I want a kiss. Miss you!

Love always,
Jenny

6

Spencer was back at the slaughter pad with two of Juan's pushers that he and Tic had snatched up from 34th Street. Both victims were naked and lying on a metal table, scared to death and unsure of what to expect from their abductors.

Spencer and Tic walked into the building, wearing protective bodysuits over their clothes. The two middle-aged men in their forties looked at Spencer and Tic, and shit their pants when they saw Spencer with a fillet knife in his hand. Neither of the Mexican men spoke English, and they were not only Juan's pushers but also his M-13 gang brothers.

"My amigo!" Spencer shouted as he came closer to the first man, who was badly shaking.

Spencer laid the fillet knife down on the table and then inspected his first victim like a doctor would inspect a patient. He grabbed hold of the man's hand and saw that he had all his fingernails cut down except his pinky finger.

"Coke, amigo?" Spencer asked while tapping the Mexican's pinky finger. "We'll take care of that real soon, amigo," Spencer said as he walked down to the end of the table and inspected the Mexican's feet.

"Bad feet, amigo!" Spencer said. "Right, Tic?"

"Them muthafuckas look like a cave man gone wild. I say we get rid of them!" Tic said, tossing Spencer a pair of needle-nose pliers.

"I think that'd be a great idea," Spencer said as he placed the pliers near the man's big toe, gripped the nail, and then yanked it entirely off.

"Mmmm!" the man cried out in devastating pain behind the duct tape.

"Ouch!" Tic exclaimed, before bursting out into laughter when he saw shit oozing from beneath the Mexican.

"Someone can't hold their bowels, huh, Tic?" Spencer asked.

"He's rotten!" Tic said, fanning the reek of pure shit.

When Spencer took a look at his second victim, he saw that he was badly sweating and trembling.

"Damn! We're not even to you, esé, and you're shaking like a damn fish. You're 'bout to learn not to anticipate my plans, fucker!" Spencer screamed as he grabbed the fillet knife and walked over to the second man bound to the table.

Spencer looked the man up and down and stopped at his cock. A smirk swept across Spencer's face. He grabbed the man's cock, put the fillet knife to it, and stripped the skin off to the cock head.

"Mmmm!" the Mexican cried loudly behind the duct tape.

Spencer lowered his head to the Mexican's ear and whispered, "Where do I find Juan and Mario?"

Spencer snatched the duct tape covering the man's mouth.

"Nooo! Me no English! No English!"

"Oh, so we no English, huh? I hate when you fuckers do that!" Spencer said as he replaced the duct tape back over the man's mouth.

"I feel bad for you, esé!" Tic said as he watched Spencer grab the pliers again.

"So you don't know Juan, huh? No English!" Spencer said as he began yanking off the man's toenails.

"Mmmmm!"

"I know, amigo. It hurts so badly!" Spencer mocked the man, who quickly passed out from the pain.

When Spencer saw that the man was out cold, he turned to the other captive behind him. He pulled the tape from over the man's mouth.

"Please tell me that you know where to find Juan," Spencer said to the man, who didn't comprehend anything Spencer was saying.

"No English!" the man exclaimed. "Please! No English. No—"

Before he could finish begging for his life, Spencer slashed the man in the throat, instantly killing him by crushing his larynx. Spencer then reached beneath his protective suit and grabbed a buck knife from the waist of his jeans.

"One more time, amigo!" Spencer said to the now conscious Mexican behind him.

The look in the man's eyes told Spencer that he too was ready to die for speaking no English. Spencer snatched the tape from his mouth.

"Tell me where the fuck is Juan! Your fucking boss!"

"Me no English. No compren—!"

The Mexican was dead before he could get another word out. Spencer had sliced his throat open from ear to ear.

"Tic!" Spencer called out. "Call Johnson and Miller, and have them get rid of them."

"Yes sir, boss. Everything taken care of," Tic replied.

* * *

"Yellow! Hey, man, we need some of that good shit!" Ham said to Banga.

"Where?"

"Over here on 5th Street in front of Jake's store," Ham gave his location and order in code.

"I'm on 8th Street. Give me a second. Sue's on his way. He's already down there. He's busy with Stacy's ass right now," Banga said.

"He still fucking with Real, huh?" Ham asked, calling Stacy by her nickname.

"Yeah! Throwback pussy don't never get old. Let me see if he's done. I'll get back at you cuzo," Banga said.

"Okay, cuzo. Hit me back up," Ham said as he disconnected the phone.

Bang was in the trap house on 8th Street getting his groove on with a beautiful Puerto Rican bitch named Quinny.

"That's right, baby, eat that dick!" Banga said to her as she was sucking his dick while he lay back in bed and called Sue Rabbit.

Sue Rabbit's phone rang twice before he picked it up. "What they do, Yellow?"

"I need them real soon," Banga reminded Sue.

"I'm around the corner from you now."

"Okay, give me a minute. When you pull up, there are two lil niggas out there named Jess and Adam. Tell them to hit up the trap on 2nd Street," Banga instructed.

"Alright! I see them now," Sue Rabbit said as he hung up the phone.

Banga grabbed Quinny by the back of her head and began fucking her mouth until he shot his load down her throat.

"I love you, papi!"

"You love my money, dick, and head, not me!"

"Whatever, dumbass nigga!" Quinny said, throwing a pillow in Banga's face before she rushed to the bathroom to get ready for work.

Banga walked outside where he met up with Sue Rabbit stepping out of his Caprice Bubble with two duffel bags in his hands.

"Same as last night—twenty. Smooth said to bring the money if you come. If not, he'll be making a trip in two weeks to go re-up."

"Yellow," Banga said as he quickly took the bags inside.

He removed two kilos of cocaine after putting the rest of the kilos in a hidden safe under the kitchen sink.

Banga called Ham's phone and got him after the first ring.

"Yo!"

"Yo my ass, nigga. Let's get to work. Come get this shit!" Banga said as he hung up his phone.

* * *

After the close call on his life, Smooth was no longer fond of meeting and doing business with Stone out in the open. Stone and Smooth had developed a close relationship after Smooth learned how Stone had retaliated and cleaned out his truck when he got shot. Smooth could have been sitting in prison if Metro-Dade would have found the drugs and guns inside. When Stone tried to pay him the money he owed Smooth for the drugs, Smooth refused to accept it and told him that it was on the house.

"You looked out for me, man. I could be doing fed time right now," Smooth said as he took a sip of Jamaican rum that Stone had convinced him to drink as a guest gift.

China sat intertwined with Smooth and let him drink as much as he wanted. She was doing the driving, and they were going straight home after Smooth wrapped up business with Stone.

"So, mon, tin tings on tin I need," Stone said, informing Smooth of his much-needed supply and increased quantity.

"You want ten on top of ten?" Smooth asked Stone, who then stood up and walked to his bar to pour himself another drink.

"Exactly mon—twenty."

"I got you, Stone. I'll shoot you ten now and another ten in the morning. Is that okay?"

"It's wonderful, mon!" Stone said as he briefly walked out of the room.

"Are you okay, baby?" China asked Smooth, who she knew was fucked up.

"Yeah!" Smooth replied sluggishly.

"Give me this!" she said as she reached under his T-shirt and down into his pants, removing his Glock .22 and placing it inside her Coach bag.

"We good, baby!" he said as he leaned in to kiss China.

It was a sloppy, drunk kiss, but China appreciated it.

Stone came back into the living room with two duffel bags full of money. Lately, the temptation of getting back into the game with Smooth was high for China. But she vowed never to go back to prison. Smooth was doing a great job; however, they rarely spent time together. He was either out at one of his trap houses all night until morning, or he'd be too exhausted when he got home to give China a good fuck. Or he was on the run just to be on the run.

"The money's all dare, mon!" Stone said as he dropped the duffel bags on the floor next to Smooth's feet.

"Baby, go get them bags out the truck," Smooth directed China.

China wanted to cuss out Smooth's ass because she was serious about not having anything more to do with the game, including trafficking any form of drugs. She got up and walked out to Smooth's new Range Rover and retrieved the duffel bags.

"I got something for his ass when we get home, for this. He gonna know that when I say no, it means no!" she said to herself.

When China walked back into the house, she saw Smooth drinking another glass of rum. "Here you go, Stone."

"Thank you, gal," Stone said, grabbing the duffel bags from China.

"In thee morning, make sure thee mon remember me!" Stone reminded.

"I will make sure he calls you. Come on, Smooth. Let's go. Enough of this Jamaican rum!" she said as she took the glass out of his hand and helped him to his feet.

Damn! I'm fucked up! Smooth thought when he stood up and the room began to spin.

"Damn, mon! Can you walk? Me carry you if you need!" Stone offered.

China didn't like this at all. *Who gets their connect inebriated, and why?* she thought.

China then grabbed the duffel bags and allowed Stone to help walk Smooth out to the car.

Man! I can't believe that shit fucked me up like this! Smooth thought as he was helped into the passenger-side seat of his SUV.

"Thanks a lot, Stone. Next time, please limit him to one drink!" China told Stone, who started laughing at her.

Stone liked China a lot.

"Okay, I will make sure he only drinks one drink," he agreed as China pulled off.

While China drove them home, Tracy came to her mind. China had planned to surprise Smooth on his birthday with a threesome. She was falling for Tracy, and she couldn't believe how close they had gotten in such little time.

I can't wait until he meets her, she thought as she came to a red light at an intersection.

"I love you, China!" Smooth said sluggishly while rubbing on her thigh and trying to get his feel on.

China grabbed Smooth's hand and helped him get under her miniskirt. She placed his hand on her pussy but then removed it.

"None for you tonight! I told you to leave me out of your business," China said to a mumbling Smooth.

"Amanda, you tripping!" Smooth said, not realizing that he called China another woman's name.

China's rejection had caused him immediately to think about another woman.

"My name is China Preston last time I checked, but I'ma let you have that one, Smooth!" she said, a bit hurt inside, but she didn't allow his snub to get her worked up.

When China pulled up to their apartment complex, she turned off the Range Rover after cracking the windows. Without saying a word, China exited the SUV and left a passed-out Smooth inside. She ran into Miranda getting off the elevator.

"Hey, China. How are you?"

"I'm okay, Miranda. Just taking it slow. What 'bout you?"

"I'm okay. Just exhausted. Long day at work today. How are you and Smooth getting along?"

"Oh, he's in the car probably asleep."

"In the car? Are y'all alright?" Miranda inquired.

"Yeah! We're fine," China lied. "He'll be up once he gets sober."

"Okay. Well, I'll see you later."

"Okay, nice seeing you," China said as she walked over toward her and Smooth's apartment.

Once inside, China fed Zorro, showered, and then lay in bed thinking of all the women who Smooth had probably slept with while she was in prison. She couldn't help but wonder if he was seeing any of them still. He called her 'Amanda,' and China knew that Amanda was the cook girl.

What else do we have in common? China wanted to know.

She would see what he had to say once he sobered up. Meantime, China called Tracy to come over.

"Hello?"

"Come over. I need someone to hold me tonight," China pleaded into her phone.

"Where's Smooth?" Tracy asked.

"Fuck Smooth! I don't want to talk about him. You coming over or not?"

"I'm coming now, baby," Tracy answered.

* * *

Pascal and Mario had been watching the two workers on 26th Street for Smooth for about thirty minutes. They were hustling nonstop on the corner.

"These Negros getting money, esé!" Pascal said to Mario, who was sitting on the passenger side of the all-black Charger.

"You ready?" Mario asked.

"Always ready, homes!" Pascal answered.

"Let's go!"

Pascal and Mario exited the Charger and ran toward the two workers. Their backs were turned as they leaned into a car window while making a drug sale. When Pascal and Mario got close, one of the men turned around, since he sensed trouble. Before he could reach for his weapon or warn his partner, Pascal blew off his entire face with his double-barrel Mossberg pump.

Boom! Boom!

Mario took the second worker down by hitting him twice in the back of the head. The fiend quickly got out of sight after seeing both murders. He was happy, because he had also run off with the workers' dope.

It was only midnight, and Pascal and Mario had one more block to go drop off whatever belonged to Smooth.

"Let's go to 103rd, esé. Premo tells me there are some Negros pushing all day," Mario exclaimed.

* * *

"Umm, shit!" China purred as she came to her climax.

Tracy ate her pussy like a professional porn star. Bad as she hated to admit, Tracy ate her pussy better than Smooth.

She couldn't say "other men" because she had only been with Smooth.

After Tracy continued to suck on China's clit, China grabbed Tracy by her ponytail and began gyrating her hips, fucking Tracy's face. She felt herself coming again.

"Uhhh, shit! I'm coming!" China moaned loudly as she squirted all over Tracy's face. "Yes, baby!" she continued breathlessly.

China quickly rolled off the bed and attached a twelve-inch dildo strap.

"Put that ass in the air!" China ordered.

"Yes, baby!" Tracy replied and did as she was told.

When she was on all fours, China climbed back in bed, grabbed Tracy by her hips, and then plunged deeply inside her wet pussy.

"Ohh, baby! Yes! Fuck me, China!" Tracy cried in ecstasy.

China fucked Tracy all the way until dawn and then let Tracy go home. China then showered, cleaned the room so Smooth wouldn't see the sex evidence, and made breakfast. When Smooth walked up to the apartment, he was hit with the redolence of China's delicious breakfast. When he called for her, she had already gone to work.

7

*A*fter dropping off the extra ten bricks for Stone, Smooth headed over to the trap to see how things were holding up. When he pulled up, he saw Sue Rabbit's Caprice with new rims. He got out of his truck and walked up to the door, just as Sue was opening the door to let him in.

"What's up, my nigga?" Sue Rabbit said to Smooth.

"Just chilling, man. How's everything going?"

"Business is fast, and product is low, and two of our workers are dead!" Sue explained.

"Who are they?"

"Travis and Danny," Sue Rabbit said.

"Ain't no one see nothing?"

"Nothing! But we already know who it is. It happened on 26th, and then early this morning, three more niggas got killed on 103rd," Sue Rabbit informed Smooth.

"Damn, we got to call a meeting today and find out how we can pay for their funerals. It's the least I can do," Smooth said. "Far as product, do you have enough to hold you for two days?"

"Yeah, I got enough to hold me for two days."

"Alright, so where is Guru?" Smooth asked.

"He busy picking up the money from the traps."

"That's wonderful. Let's go get some breakfast. I already ate. I just want to treat you, feel me?" Smooth said.

"Shit! Let's go. I'ma call one of our workers to keep an eye on the trap," Sue said as he called up Mall.

"What's up, Sue?"

"I need you to keep an eye on the trap. I'm about to step out for a minute."

Mall was just down the road already, keeping an eye out for suspicious activity.

"Okay. Shit, you know I'm here, bro," Mall said.

"Good. Good. See ya later," Sue Rabbit said before hanging up the phone. "Who's car we taking?"

"You know two niggas in your toy will look like straight dope boys."

"Yeah, I know. That's why that bitch for sale!"

"Nah, I can't go for that!" Smooth exclaimed while walking to his Range Rover. "How much you selling it for?"

"$40,000," Sue Rabbit replied.

"I'll buy it," Smooth responded sincerely.

"When and why?"

"Why is my business. When? Later on today," Smooth told him.

"Alright."

"Sue, I want you to know that I appreciate you and Guru for always looking out."

"Always, bro!" Sue said.

"When y'all niggas had no clue when I would jump, y'all went to hit a lick and robbed the Mexican just to keep business running," Smooth said, making a quick left onto 86th.

"I don't ever want y'all to struggle if I'm not around, so we gonna keep extra product put up. Today, I'ma show only you my connect to the cooking. You are to bring nobody with you. Nobody!" he emphasized.

"I got you, bro," Sue Rabbit said as they pulled up to Roxy's restaurant.

* * *

"China! Smooth's here!" Roxy screamed for China, who was working in the back chopping up potatoes.

So what! What the hell does he want? He must be on some guilt trip! China thought as she continued to work. She was on her last three potatoes. *Can't he wait!*

"Girl! Who is that nigga he be with? It's the second time I've seen them together. That nigga is fine too," China's friend Jane, who was washing and cutting collard greens alongside China, said.

"Girl, since we been home, yo pussy been a hot commodity. Every nigga you fuck, you leave 'em the next morning. Slow your ass down. You see Tabby got a steady man. Shit! Be like her and stick to one nigga, before one of these niggas gives you something that you can't get rid of!" China said to Jane.

"I already got something that I can't get rid of—good head and pussy!"

China erupted in laughter.

"And ass if the mood's right!"

"Bitch! You is stupid!" China said after laughing and wiping her teary eyes.

When China walked out into the dining room, she found Roxy sitting at the table with Smooth and his homeboy, who was flirting with Roxy. China knew when her sister was in heat like a female dog.

"What's up, baby?" China asked Smooth, who was drinking a Coke.

"Just stopping by to see what you were up to," Smooth replied.

He stood up and embraced China and then gave her a peck on the cheek.

"Sorry for getting fucked up. I know that's why you let me sleep in the truck. Seriously, I'm sorry, baby."

He don't even remember calling me another bitch's name! China thought.

"It's okay. I got a break in a few minutes," China said.

"Baby, this is my homeboy, Sue Rabbit."

"Hey, Sue Rabbit."

"Hello, China. Nice meeting you."

"I'm not always nice," China said.

"That's okay. Nobody is!" Sue joked.

"Roxy, can I go for my break now?" China asked Roxy, who was mesmerized and gawking at Sue Rabbit.

"Yeah, half an hour."

"Great. Come on, Smooth. Tell your friend that you'll see him in thirty minutes."

"Shit! You already told him!" Smooth said.

As China and Smooth walked out the front door toward his truck, Tracy looked on with extreme jealousy. She knew that China was going to get her a quick fuck, and she badly wanted to be a part of it.

Smooth is a good-looking guy, but China is my bitch, and I'll soon have her make up her mind, Tracy thought while staring daggers at Smooth's Range Rover. *I know how to get rid of him.*

If anyone in the city knew where to find Juan, it was Tracy, who used to date him, until he cheated on her.

Bingo! Tracy thought.

* * *

Italian Seafood on South Beach was a nice luxurious restaurant. When Guru stepped through the door with Landi on his arm, the smell of fried shrimp lingered.

"Place smells good, Landi," Guru stated, with a grumbling stomach.

"I love this place."

They took their seats on opposite sides of the table. Guru wanted to look in her eyes and admire her stunning beauty.

"So, what do you want to eat?" she asked.

"Wait a minute! Let me set this straight. I'm paying the bill. So you tell me what you want to eat, beautiful," Guru announced.

"Is it a man's pride that a woman can't pay for your meal?"

"Landi, baby, what do you want?" Guru asked her again, with a smile on his face.

"Stop looking like that. It turns me off!" Landi said as a joke.

"What do you want me to look like, huh?"

"I'm only kidding. I love your smile and gangsta look," she replied as she picked up the menu to order.

"Welcome to Italian Seafood. Are you ready to order?" a waitress asked.

Damn! Guru thought as he checked out the beautiful Italian server. He was glad that Landi's focus was on ordering and not where his eyes were at the moment.

"We'll take the *fra diavolo* and two glasses of 2004 Bell Epoque rosé champagne," Landi said.

"Okay, ma'am. We will be right with you. Do you want ice in the champagne? It's already chilled."

"No, just chilled."

"Okay," the server said and then left.

"What the fuck is her problem? Ice in champagne? Where do they do that?" Landi exclaimed.

"Maybe she's on drugs?'

"Yeah, right!" Landi said.

"So, are you enjoying yourself?" Guru asked.

"Are you really asking me if I'm enjoying my time with you?"

"That too!"

"I'm loving every moment with my new friend, if that's what you want to know," Landi said seductively.

"As long as you are enjoying being in the presence of a real man, then everything is okay," Guru said.

Guru was feeling Landi, and he had made up his mind that if she wanted more out of just being friends, then he was going to cash in his player chips. Good girls like Landi were not easy to come by in life. There was always a woman out there for a man who knew what loyalty was, and that's what Guru seriously wanted in his life.

I'm not interested in a woman who is ready to fuck the next man just because, Guru thought.

Landi and Guru had gotten deep into each other's personal lives. Despite talking on the phone daily, seeing each other in person was another thing. Landi knew that Guru was a drug dealer, killer, and gentleman. But she didn't care. Guru was her type, and she definitely had a thing for bad guys like him.

* * *

Tina and Ham were happy soon-to-be parents. Ham knew that he was taking a risk by being with Tina, knowing that she had another year until she turned eighteen. But Ham didn't care. He met her on the streets and felt that he saved her from drugs. The night she decided to quit smoking crack and clean up her life was a good thing for both of them. Her parents had left her for dead, so Ham prohibited her from any type of association with them.

"Daddy, I love you!" Tina said to Ham as they were cuddling up cozy in bed.

"I love you too, beautiful," Ham agreed as he leaned over to give her a kiss.

"So tell me. If it's a boy, what are you going to name him?" Ham asked.

"I would love to name him after you as a junior, but I don't want the police messing with you," Tina explained.

"Fuck the police! They are not going to sweat that shit. You a black—"

"No, Ham! I'm not taking any chances. If our child's a boy, we will make him a junior. I'll be eighteen next year. Let's just not get them folks in our business," she begged.

Ham turned her on her back and softly kissed her lips. He understood exactly where she was coming from and was only testing her to see where her head was.

"I love you, baby. Ain't no system will ever get between us, okay?" Ham said.

"Yes, daddy," Tina purred when Ham slid his cock inside her.

"I love you too, Ham," Tina said as she kissed him deeply as he made love to her.

Tina had never had a man love her just for who she was. Since the age of thirteen, she'd been giving her body to older men in exchange for crack. Ham was different. He saw potential in her that no man before him saw. Ham was her official first love. He had the power to make her and break her.

* * *

Amanda heard the knocks at her door after stepping out of a soothing shower.

"I'm coming," she shouted as she quickly dried off and then slid on a pair of sweatpants and a sports bra.

The visitors continued to knock persistently.

Who the fuck is this knocking like they don't have no sense? Amanda wanted to know.

When she got to the door and opened it, she saw Smooth standing there with a man who she had never met.

"Sorry, but I'm in a hurry, and I didn't think you heard me."

"Come in, Smooth. You and your friend," Amanda said as she stepped out of the way.

"Amanda, meet my second-in-command, Sue Rabbit. This is Amanda, our cook," Smooth introduced.

The look on Amanda's face revealed perplexity.

"What's this? Are you sending him instead of you now?" Amanda asked, with a hint of attitude.

Smooth smiled, knowing exactly what was going through her head. He walked up to her and grabbed her in an embrace and then kissed her on her lips.

"Nah, baby, when he comes, just handle what he need done, okay?"

Amanda looked at Smooth and then at Sue Rabbit, who had just sat down on her sofa.

"Okay, Smooth. So you're not running away?"

"Never will I run away. Real friends don't abandon their friends, right?" Smooth asked.

"Yeah," Amanda said.

"Sue Rabbit's gonna drop off the next drop we need cooked up. Only him, and no one else will be coming with him."

"Just him?"

"Only him!" Smooth reiterated.

"Well, I'ma be looking for a new place to cook at. I just got some neighbors, and they look too damn nosy," Amanda explained.

"I have two apartments that I can let you work out of on 133rd. Pick one, and it's yours!" Smooth offered.

"Thanks, Smooth."

"No. Thank you, baby!" Smooth said as he and Sue left her apartment. "See you in a couple of days," Smooth said outside the door.

"Okay," Amanda said as she shut the door.

"Damn, she's like a fucking model, bro. China bad too. But her! Damn, bro! You be cuffing for real," Sue Rabbit exclaimed.

"Something like that. We stopped all sexual ties when China came home. Yeah right!"

"I saw how you were holding her, nigga. Y'all was making my dick hard!" Sue Rabbit admitted.

"Nigga! Roxy was making yo' dick hard!" Smooth replied. "By the way, what's up with you and her?"

"I got her number. I know she was digging the boy."

"Yo! Hold up," Smooth said as he got to the truck and felt his phone vibrate in his pocket.

"What's up?"

"Yo, this Mac!"

"I know. So what's good?"

"I'ma need ten of them tonight. Will that be okay, pal?"

"Of course, bro. If you got the money, I got the product," Smooth answered.

"Ten-four!" Mac said as he hung up.

"Bro, ya birthday's in three days. I know we gone do it big, my nigga!" Sue Rabbit said.

"Hell yeah. If China don't have any other plans."

"Boy, China got yo' ass in check. Don't think I don't see that shit, bro."

"Nigga, whatever!" Smooth exclaimed, laughing.

"Okay!" Sue Rabbit said.

In all truth, what Sue Rabbit was really seeing was a totally different person than the China who Smooth had known his entire childhood.

She was his baby, and he loved her to death. But since day one after waking up in the hospital, he found himself loving a completely different China. She was more of a grown woman, with more sense to stay risk-free from anything that would hinder her freedom again.

After earlier having a quickie in his truck while on her break, China again pleaded for Smooth to leave the game alone. True enough, he had been stacking his paper and had enough at just eighteen years old to retire, but he had his niggas to think about. Further, he wouldn't sleep well until Juan José and Mario Lopez—his enemies—were six feet deep.

8

*A*fter dropping off Sue Rabbit back at the trap, Smooth had a meeting to attend, where he was the top man in charge. When he pulled up to Spencer's beach house on South Beach, he espied the peaceful environment and thought about seeking a beach house for him and China.

"It's nice as hell out here, Spencer," Smooth complimented as he walked through the door.

"It's nice, isn't it? They have a couple for lease down the road," Spencer said.

"I swear, you and me think just alike," Smooth replied.

"What? You already considering?"

"Hell yeah! The moment I seen yo shit!" Smooth said as he walked into the living room with Spencer and saw his second attendant.

"Tic?" Smooth asked.

"Yeah, that's me!" Tic said as he stood up and offered his hand.

Smooth shook it and sat down on the sofa.

"So, what's good?" Smooth asked as Spencer brought him a glass of Hennessy.

"Well," Spencer began as he lay back in his La-Z-Boy, "these Mexicans are too damn loyal. Every one of them died with the same words."

"What are they saying?"

"No English. Please, no English!" Spencer emphasized.

"Basically, Mr. José has put the fear of God in these men; for even in death, they refuse to give up this man," Tic added.

Smooth killed his drink, raised up from the plush sofa, and demanded, "Well, start snatching women along with the men!"

Spencer looked at Tic, who had an impish smirk on his face. He could tell that Tic was already loving Smooth. Since his sister Rebecca's death, Spencer and Smooth had become very close. Spencer didn't know Sue Rabbit, but his loyalty would soon lead him to meet the second man in charge of the streets.

Smooth had seen too much cutthroat in his life to put all his eggs in the same basket. He had killers who didn't know about the other killers. After reading an urban book written by Trayvon D. Jackson entitled *Kings of Pawn*, Smooth was up on the game of how every smile wasn't a smile and how every killer was a real nigga. A nigga would play up under you. Just like your money, every Benjamin wasn't a Benjamin. Smooth had two separate armies shedding blood in his name.

After leaving Spencer's place, Smooth went back to his apartment. China wasn't home yet. He showered and then got dressed in all black. He quickly slapped himself together a sloppy sandwich and then walked over to Miranda's. After knocking on the door twice, she answered wearing only a bra and boy shorts. Smooth had almost forgotten why he had stopped by as he stood mesmerized by her sexy body.

"Back to earth! It's not polite to stare!" Miranda said as she walked away from the door.

Smooth's dick became hard watching her ass jiggle.

"Come on in. I'll put on some clothes."

"You're alright. Why you doing that?"

"Because you have a lady, Smooth, and this is not respectful," she replied. "Plus, we are not on that level for you to enjoy the sight of what you're seeing right now."

Miranda then stormed off to change.

"I respect that," Smooth said to himself as Miranda disappeared into the back room.

When she returned, Smooth was sitting on the sofa.

"So, what's up?" she asked.

"Miranda, do you think you could help me find a nice home?"

"Have I ever let you down?"

"Nah, and I appreciate that. You've been a real friend and female mentor to me. I just don't know how to repay you," Smooth admitted.

"You've already repaid me, Smooth, with real friendship. I just want to tell you something. You have a good woman. She's not the woman I seen leave here years ago."

"You see it too, huh?"

"Of course I do. It's called growing up, Smooth. Now you have to grow up with her before you lose her."

"China will never leave me," Smooth told her.

"Stop being naive, Smooth, and open your eyes!"

What the fuck does that mean! he wondered.

Miranda was aware of the suspicious girl coming around a lot, and even caught China and her kissing one night in the parking lot.

"Why do you say I need to open my eyes?" Smooth asked.

Miranda stood up and walked to the bar. She fixed both of them a glass of Remy and Coke.

"Smooth, the other night as well as last night, China's girlfriend . . . !"

"Girlfriend? Man, China don't have no girlfriend!" Smooth cut in.

Miranda sucked her teeth, grabbed her iPhone, and pulled up pictures she had taken of China and Tracy making out in the parking lot. "Look for yourself!" she said as she tossed her phone over to him.

When Smooth looked at the pictures, his heart dropped when he saw China kissing another woman, who he didn't know from Eve. "Who is she?"

"You'll have to hire a private investigator for that. I do real estate, sir," Miranda said sarcastically. "But like I said, you have to get a grip on yourself and not give her a reason to leave, Smooth."

"That's why I like you, Miranda. You keep it too real."

"And I want you to keep it real too. Please don't blow up and expose me, because I don't want no trouble," Miranda said.

"I got you," Smooth replied as he stood up to leave.

"Just find me a nice home, and see if you can find me some more apartments," Smooth requested as he walked toward the front door.

"I will get in touch with you tomorrow, Smooth."

"Call me, Miranda. Oh, and one more thing before I go."

"You want me to watch Zorro," Miranda answered before he could ask the question.

"Yeah! I'm going out of town in the morning, and I'm taking China."

"I will watch him, honey. Just knock on the door," Miranda said.

"Okay," Smooth replied as he walked back to his apartment.

I can't believe China is hiding her lil boo thing from me. That's crazy. I'ma see how long it takes her to inform me. Shit, she doing her! I ain't a man if I don't do my shit, Smooth thought as he looked at the time. It was 5:45 p.m.

China will get off work at 6:00 p.m., and I'ma be in some pussy, Smooth thought as he pulled out his phone and called a woman that he just couldn't get enough of.

"Hello!"

"I'm on my way. When you open that door up, I don't want to see no clothes on!"

"Boy, stop playing!" Amanda said.

"I'm dead serious," Smooth responded before he hung up.

When Smooth got back home, Zorro began following him around and crying. Smooth then watched as his dog ate yet continued to cry. Smooth knew why. Zorro wanted to go out for a walk.

"I don't have time right now. I gotta go handle something, buddy!" Smooth said to Zorro.

It wasn't long before Smooth showed up at Amanda's place. Just like he requested, she answered the door wearing nothing but a smile.

"Damn, baby! You just too beautiful," he said as he walked inside, taking Amanda into his arms and kissing her.

He closed the door with his foot and pulled her to the plush carpet. He sucked on her tits and caressed them passionately.

"Uhhh, baby!" Amanda purred, pulling Smooth's shirt and vest over his head, knocking off his hat.

For the first time, she felt part of his missing ear when she caressed his head, which made her shed a tear. She pulled him down and gently kissed him on the remainder of his ear.

"Baby, you are doing something to me. I could play number two real good. I don't want to steal her spot if it's not for me, but please let me be number two," Amanda begged.

"I will, baby. Now give me this pussy!" Smooth said as he took off his pants.

Amanda then spread her legs and let Smooth enter her world deeply.

"Yes, daddy!" Amanda purred, arching her back. "Beat this pussy!" she demanded, which is exactly what Smooth did.

9

"Jenny Davis! You have a visit!" the female guard announced over the PA system.

Jenny couldn't believe her ears, and neither could others in the day room.

"Girl, you done finally got you a visit!" Jenny's homegirl Carlisha said.

Carlisha backed Jenny in every altercation. She was from Tallahassee and called herself "Savage."

"Yeah, it's surprising. Do you think it's China?" Jenny asked as they walked to her cell.

"It could be. You won't know until you get up there, girl. Make sure you take some pictures," Carlisha suggested.

"I will."

As Jenny pulled off her clothes in a hurry, Carlisha stood at the door and watched her, admiring Jenny's sexy body. When Jenny turned around, she caught Carlisha gawking at her body.

"What?" Jenny said shyly and blushing.

"You're fine as hell, woman!"

"You are too. The good thing is, you're mine, right?" Jenny asked, putting on her visitation clothes.

"Of course."

"Well, then be here when I get back tonight. I want that good-ass head you got," Jenny said as she walked passed her.

Carlisha didn't have to be asked to watch over Jenny's cell.

Since China had been dropping her money every two months, Jenny could pay for anything she wanted. Her respect level increased dramatically. Anyone who got on her shit list was called out to the cell and beat down by her goon, Carlisha.

When Jenny stepped into the visitation room, she immediately saw China. China stood up, hugged her, and gave her a quick kiss.

"Girl, you're getting thick as a snicker."

"Shit! You're the cause of it!"

"How much your ass weigh?" China asked, loving the new booty, hips, and thighs on Jenny.

China's pussy was getting wet just imagining how Jenny would taste when she came home.

"I fucking miss you, girl," Jenny said.

"And I miss you more."

"Do you miss me or the taste of this phat pussy?" Jenny asked.

"Both!" China fired back.

China then slid Jenny a hot eighteen-wheeler, a cold Coke, and a bag of chips.

"I know you have a locker full of bullshit, but I still wanted to grab you something," China said.

"Thank you, China."

"Welcome, honey."

"So, how are you and Smooth getting along?"

"I guess we're okay."

"What do you mean by that? I thought you were ready to see him?"

"It's not the same, and I don't know if it's me or him. I mean—" China stopped, raising her arms in the air "—I love him, but I feel that his street life and love for his homeboys is too much, Jenny." After a moment, she continued, "Then I met this girl at my job named Tracy!"

A surprised expression appeared on Jenny's face.

"Don't look like that. She's gone when you come home," China lied.

"She better be!" Jenny said, giving China a serious look.

"But like I was saying, Tracy and me have been kicking it. By the way, she's the one taking the pictures. But, yeah, I feel that Smooth is also still seeing his bitches."

"Really? That's so fucked up! What makes you think that?" Jenny asked.

"The other night he was so damn drunk, and he called me another bitch's name."

"And you didn't do shit?" Jenny inquired as she took a sip of her soda and bite of the sandwich.

"The bitch's name he called out was his cook girl, so I didn't blow up in speculation," China explained.

"China, don't set yourself up to get hurt. I know that Smooth is all you know. But there are some good men."

"I don't want another man, Jenny. If I do leave Smooth, it won't be for a man!" China said with emotion cracking in her voice, which Jenny espied.

Jenny quickly dropped her sandwich and reached for China's hand. "Baby, what are you saying?"

"I'm saying that my interest in men is not there at the moment," China admitted as she turned her head away, right as a tear fell. "He's all I know, Jenny. I just want him to get out of the game before he gets himself killed," she cried.

Hearing China's confession of not having any interest in men wasn't surprising. Jenny knew the percentage of women who got released from prison and lost interest in men.

She was a victim herself. Before she allowed China to turn her out, Jenny's heart was on her childhood boyfriend. The more China sexed her, the more eradicated her love became for her boyfriend back home. Jenny bridled her excitement of hearing China's confession. She had China, and she would prove to her that she was the only person she needed.

"Baby, just a couple more years. Just wait on me, and I promise we will get married and it will all be about us," Jenny told China, who shook her head up and down.

"Okay," China said softly. "Let's take a picture. I have to run shortly. He's in the car waiting on me," China explained.

"So when will you tell him about Tracy?" Jenny inquired as they walked hand in hand toward the camera girl.

"Oh his birthday. We're planning a threesome."

"You and Tracy and Smooth?"

"Yeah!"

"Wow!" Jenny said, surprised.

* * *

"Yes! Ummm! Fuck me, papi!" Tracy screamed out in ecstasy as Juan fucked her hard in her asshole.

Tracy was on all fours, gripping the silk sheets on her bed, with her head buried partially in her pillow. They both were sweaty and inebriated from the Remy Martin and Coke.

"Good ass, mama!" Juan complimented her as he slowed his pace to hang in a while longer.

When Tracy called Juan's phone, he was shocked to hear from her. After their decision to separate, Juan and she had said nothing to each other for almost a year.

"You like papi's dick?" he asked as he sped up his penetration, trying to explode intensively.

"Yes! I like papi's dick!"

Damn, Juan. Hurry the fuck up! This shit is hurting now! Tracy thought as the pleasure began to turn to pain.

"Arrghhh!" Juan exploded inside her ass.

"Thank you, Jesus!"

"What? Keep Jesus out of this, mama!" Juan stated as he watched her hop up from the bed and rush to the bathroom to get rid of his seed in her ass. "Mama's ass still good," he said as he collapsed on the bed.

When Tracy emerged from a soothing shower and came back into the room, Juan was completely passed out. She was intoxicated, but not tore out the frame like he was. She climbed back into bed and playfully slapped him on his face. He mumbled as he came out of his sleep ready to go wild.

Shell shock, she thought.

"We need to talk, Juan."

"What's up, mama? Me exhausted."

"Yeah, me too, but I'm not talking 'bout fucking."

"So what is it, bonita?" he asked.

"I know where to find a man you're looking for," Tracy told Juan, who immediately became extra attentive, best as he could propping up on his elbow.

"Who are you talking about?"

Tracy smiled at Juan as she straddled him, rubbed his chest, and began to play with his curly fuzz.

"His name is Smooth," Tracy began as the smile on Juan's face began to disappear.

"Oh really, mama!"

"Yes, but there are some serious stipulations," she demanded.

"Tell me, mama. Papi listening."

* * *

When Smooth pulled up to Jefe's luxurious home in New York, he tapped China on her thigh, since she was asleep in the passenger seat. "We're here, baby."

"Damn! I was knocked out, huh?" China said.

"Yeah, snoring like a damn grizzly bear."

"Whatever, Smooth!" China said with a laugh. "I know you're not talking about our drive from Miami to Ocala when you sounded like one yourself."

"Yeah, yeah!" Smooth teased as he reached out the window and hit the call button.

"Come up, Smooth," Jefe's voice said.

"Alright."

"Damn! Jefe must have fired somebody. We never heard him come to his own speaker."

"There's a time for new things and old things," Smooth said.

Tell that to yourself, China thought as Smooth drove through the gate and parked behind Jefe's Rolls Royce.

"Nice car," China said.

"You like that, huh?"

"It's better than the Mercedes," she said as they stepped out together with two duffel bags filled with money.

When they walked through the front door, Raul grabbed the bags from them.

"Come, Jefe's in the library, amigo," Raul announced as he led them through the house.

Once inside, Jefe was not there as Raul had informed them. "Sorry! Last I checked, he was in here. He'll be here shortly," Raul said before he stepped out.

Smooth looked at the many books on the shelves and saw an entire shelf of Silk White and Jacob Spears. China smiled when she noticed one of Spears's books that had yet to be released.

"Come here, baby," China said, removing the book from the shelf.

Smooth strutted over to her and grabbed her from behind, looking over her shoulder at the book.

"This is book three of the series. This man writes a story similar to ours. I've been waiting for this book!" she exclaimed.

"What's our story, baby?" Smooth asked.

"Two young lovers since childhood who love each other to no limits," China gave Smooth a part of the story.

China mentioned the coincidental part about the books' main characters having their same names as well as the part where the book character of China falls for a woman.

"You two aren't making babies in my library, are you?" Jefe startled them.

"Nah, Jefe. Just checking out my favorite book."

"Oh, so you are a fan of Jacob Spears?"

"Yes, I am. Can I . . . ?"

"Yes, you can. I'm still trying to get Smooth to read Silk White."

"I'm all done, Jefe, and it's returned in the money. Plus, I want to read *Stranded*. That bitch looks fire!" Smooth said.

"Suit yourself! Just return them. Now, let's get to business. I also have a birthday gift for you."

"How did you know my birthday was coming up?" Smooth asked.

"You're not that solid that I don't know you," Jefe said.

When Smooth turned around, he instantly saw China trying to bridle her guilty conscience.

"You're such a poor faker," Smooth told her.

"So!" China replied as she began reading Spear's book.

* * *

Spencer and Tic didn't waste any time finding their next victims. They weren't at their slaughter pad this time. Instead, they knocked on the door of a small-time hustler and pretended to be Jehovah's Witnesses. Easy access was available for them. There was a total of six adult immigrants inside from Mexico. Fortunately, the children were at a homeschool teacher's house two blocks away. The three women and three men sat on the sofa in the living room unbound but naked.

"Who speaks English, say me!" Spencer announced, holding up his right hand while he held his Glock .22 in his left.

Nobody raised their hand, which made Spencer extremely mad. He aimed his Glock at the woman on the end of the sofa to his left and shot her twice in her forehead.

"The next muthafucka who wants to act crazy in here, I'ma do the same."

"Me no English!"

Boom! Boom! Boom!

Before the timorous Mexican man could plead, Spencer squeezed the trigger, taking out both he and his wife.

"Next!" Spencer screamed.

"I think the pretty one on the right may know how not to die!" Tic said, carrying a shotgun in his hand as he walked up toward her.

"Bonita, where are Juan and Mario?" Tic asked while rubbing the pretty woman's face with his gloved hand.

The woman was badly shaking, obviously afraid of losing her life.

"Señorita bonita, where are Juan and Mario?" Tic asked again.

The pretty woman shook her head from side to side and pointed at the man next to her.

"Juan," she said seriously as she repeated back to Tic.

"He Juan? So he's Juan, huh?" Tic said, growing impatient with the woman.

Tic exploded by ramming the butt of the shotgun to her grill, knocking out all her front teeth. Tic then chambered a round and shot off her entire face with two slugs. Tic was very angry.

"Somebody make Negro mad, amigos!" Spencer said as he proceeded to kill the remaining men and women.

10

Smooth and China pulled up to Banga's trap house on 8th Street and met a very happy Banga.

"Bonnie and Clyde, ten toes down—that's how I like to see y'all," Banga said.

"Yellow," Smooth said.

"What's up, China?"

"Shit! Just kicking it with my boo. So you're loving Martin County, huh?" she asked.

"This place has become a gold mine. Shit! I have a team of young hustlers getting money out here," he explained.

"So you the man in Martin, huh?" Smooth inquired.

"The man!" Banga said with emphasis.

"B-day in two days, nigga! What's on ya mind?"

"Damn! You remember too, huh?" Smooth asked in surprise.

"I know my niggas like the prints on my foot, homie."

"I like that! Well let's do this so I can get back on the road," Smooth said, grabbing his Glock .40 beneath his seat and pressing a button to his stash spot that was also under the driver's seat.

When Smooth stepped out, he lifted the entire driver's seat up and pulled a duffel bag out from a safe. After securing the stash spot, Smooth then looked at China and said, "Stay here. I won't be long."

"Okay, baby," she replied as she pulled out her iPhone to call Tracy and see what she was up to. When Smooth stepped inside the trap house, he immediately heard vague female conversation from the back. The distinctive voice of Meka could be picked out like a sore thumb.

"I didn't know Meka was here!" Smooth whispered.

"Bro, I tried everything. She knew you was coming when she heard us talking on the phone. Put this down and go holla at her."

"Nigga, China's outside. I can't do that."

"Then go tell her that. You just can't be giving cuzo good dick and then stop when wifey comes home. Meka could show out. At least back out slow," Banga advised.

"You're—"

"Smooth?" Meka said, coming into the kitchen. "Can I speak with you for a moment?"

Smooth sighed and then turned around to face Meka, who had tears in the wells of her eyes.

"I see wifey in the car. I'ma respect her, but you're not leaving here without talking with me," Meka demanded. "Try me, and I will go out there and drag the Asian off her ass, Smooth."

"Meka, there's no need to act stupid."

"Come here," she said as she walked down the hallway.

Smooth looked at Banga, who whistled. "You better hurry!"

"Watch my back, man."

"I got you, bro," Banga replied.

Smooth followed Meka to a guest room and closed the door behind him.

"Come here," she demanded, sitting on the edge of the bed.

When Smooth came closer to her, she attacked his belt and had his dick out in no time. She sucked and stroked his cock until he was fully erect. Smooth laid Meka back on the bed, pulled her skirt up to her hips, and then put her legs on his shoulders. With a strong thrust, Smooth plunged his cock deep inside of her extremely wet pussy.

"Ohhhh shit!" Meka cried out in pleasure with trembling legs. "Beat this pussy, Smooth!" Meka shouted.

* * *

"So you miss me that much?" China asked Tracy.

"Yes, I do, baby," Tracy purred while playing with her pussy.

She was glad to see China calling her. She had just hopped out of a soothing shower after a long morning and afternoon at work without China. China had Tracy in bed, slowly using a twelve-inch dildo.

"Stick it all the way in, baby, and tell me how much you love me."

"Mmmmm, China. I love you so much."

"Who's pussy is that?" China asked while rubbing her clit and praying that Smooth didn't come out and catch her.

She knew that she was pressing her luck by doing what

she was doing while he was so close by. But she promised Tracy a quickie.

"Beat that pussy like you want me to, baby! Beat that pussy!" China demanded while hearing the moans of Tracy intensify.

She knew when Tracy was about to come. "Mmmmm! I'm coming!" Tracy shouted, causing China to come to her peak.

"Shit! Ohhh! Shit, baby!" China panted as she came to her climax with Tracy. "That was good and quick," China said, wiping her pussy with a towel and rubbing her hand in some hand sanitizer.

She then sprayed a shot of her Beyoncé perfume into the air.

"He's still in there?" Tracy asked.

"Yeah, he's still in there. I wish he would hurry up."

"Did y'all have a good time?"

"Yeah, we had a good time. I can't wait until we all are together," China said.

"What do you think it's going to be like?" Tracy asked.

China looked down at her iPhone in her lap like she could see Tracy's face asking her the question.

"I don't know, Tracy. I guess how I wanted it to be with Rebecca. I can't really say how it will be until we are both there and all three of us are together," China explained.

"Would you leave me if he's not into it?"

"Hell no! Is you crazy, girl?" China asked.

"I love you."

"I love you too," China responded.

* * *

"So, when will you be back?" Meka asked, cleaning her juices from Smooth's dick with a wash rag.

"In two weeks after my birthday. I'ma be tied up, so give me two weeks. I'll be back then," Smooth promised.

"I thought you were dissing me out. Just know that I can be the sweetest person in the world and the evilest bitch from hell. The dick is good, and I've become attached. Just for you to know, I don't give these dirty dick niggas down here a chance in a day. So guess who's being the only one fucking me?" Meka said as she stood up and put her hands on her hips. "Answer me!" she demanded with a pout on her face.

Smooth leaned in and kissed her on her lips.

"Me, baby! Now I gotta go. Two weeks," Smooth reiterated, and then spun on his heels and left the room.

When he got into the living room, Banga was smoking a kush blunt while holding Smooth's duffel bag of money at the front door.

"Yo, blow some of that shit on me," Smooth asked Banga, to defuse any sex scent that may have lingered on his clothes.

Meka's pussy was scentless, but sex still has its own regulation, Smooth thought.

"I'll see you in two days," Banga said as he stepped aside to let Smooth out.

Smooth walked through the door and quickly got inside his idling Range Rover.

"Damn, baby!" China said, fanning her hands by her nose.

Oh shit! Smooth thought.

"You're smoking now?" China asked.

Damn! Close one! he considered.

"If I didn't smoke it then, baby, I won't do it now," Smooth said. "That's Banga smoking like he crazy in there. Sorry if I took long, baby."

Smooth threw a peppermint into his mouth.

"You sure, Smooth, because you look like you're guilty or high from second-hand smoke!"

"Baby, I'm okay."

"Do we need to take a piss test?"

"No!" Smooth exclaimed.

China broke out in a chuckle, causing Smooth to smirk as he navigated out of Booker Park.

"Are you hungry for some McDonald's, baby, before we get back on the road?"

"Yeah, I could go for a Big Mac," China said.

"Okay," Smooth said.

Smooth stopped at the first McDonald's, which turned out to be the only one in the small populated area in Martin County.

* * *

Javier and Tito were Juan's M-13 brothers who held down 120th and were two young seventeen-year-old killers always ready for action. Together they were driving in a

Lincoln Town Car, when they saw two of Smooth's soldiers slipping at the 7-Eleven pumping gas while chatting and not paying attention to their surroundings.

"Esé, let's flip 'em," Javier, who was sitting on the passenger side with a MAC-10 resting on his lap, said.

"Check for po-po!" Tito said as he U-turned at the light and came back toward the Seven-11.

"No po-po in sight, esé."

Tito sat at the red light three cars back, watching the two soldiers at gas pump number nine, who were unaware of the approaching threat.

"Hurry up fucking light!" Javier impatiently said, ready to squeeze, with his kill switch on high adrenaline.

"Looks like they're having the time of their lives, homes," Tito said the moment the light turned green.

"Bingo! Fucking show time!" Javier said, exhilarated, while dropping his window and pulling a blue bandana over his face.

Javier leaned out with his MAC-10 the moment one of Smooth's soldiers saw him and made a run for the backseat. Javier squeezed the trigger, hitting the slacker and dropping him to his death. He continued to shoot at the SUV they were gassing up. With an impish smirk on his face, Javier shot at the open gas tank rapidly.

Boom!

The SUV exploded into flames, causing the gas pump to explode as well. Everything and everyone in the vicinity were blown to smithereens. Smooth's soldiers had no chance.

"Got 'em, esé!" Javier shouted as he came back inside the car.

"Damn, homes. You killed everyone. We have to ditch, esé!" Tito said, turning off the highway to take back roads.

"Fuck them Negros!" Javier said, inserting a new clip into his MAC-10.

He was ready to kill more every day. Javier was so excited that he had to brag about it to someone. He picked up his iPhone and called Pascal.

"Hola?" Pascal answered.

"Two slipping at the 7-Eleven, esé. I took down the entire joint!" Javier exclaimed.

"Good, amigo! Go lay low. Feds are coming for that one, stupid. It's national already, and they're looking for a tan Lincoln Town Car."

"Oh shit, esé! Let's ditch!" Javier told Tito, who pulled behind a Walmart and wiped the steering wheel clean of his prints.

"Esé, come scoop us up. We're on 26th walking toward 30th," Javier said as he wiped his side of the car.

"Alright, esé! Me and Mario are coming," Pascal promised.

11

Club Rage was full beyond its capacity. When Smooth, China, Roxy, and Sue Rabbit emerged from the limousine, they were under the scope.

"Esé, take 'em," Pascal said to his brother, Joker, who was a skilled sharpshooter. Before he could squeeze the trigger on his sniper rifle, a big six four and 225-pound bouncer got in the way and blocked his shot.

"Fuck, esé!" Joker exclaimed, pulling the scope from his eye and going back into the SUV.

Smooth was saved by the bell with the help of the bouncer.

"The bouncer was in the way," Joker said as he watched Smooth walk into the club with his girl, China, who Juan had been informed to spare.

"We'll wait until the Negro comes out singing happy birthday, homes," Pascal told Joker.

"Remember! Spare the girlfriend!"

"Yeah, I will. Everyone else going down."

* * *

Mac had watched everything on his monitor, replaying the tape over and over.

Smooth is about to get sniped on his damn birthday, Mac thought.

He had his men on point, but he wanted to see what Smooth would want done.

"They look like they plan on sticking around," Mac said to his big-ass bodyguard, Craig.

"Yeah! They're definitely sticking around, and Smooth just took his first drink," Craig said, watching Smooth on the monitor in VIP.

"I have to let him know. Go get him, and let's see how he wants to handle the situation," Mac ordered.

"Okay, boss."

* * *

Jane and Tabby joined China in VIP with Smooth and his homeboys. Everyone was dressed to impress, wearing fly suits and dresses with expensive jewelry.

"Girl, I can't believe we in VIP!" Jane said to China over the Flo-rida emanating from the DJ's speakers that were serenading the crowd.

"Yeah, girl. Believe it and find a date!" Tabby shouted to Jane, whose eyes were on only one guy in the club.

Despite him being taken, Jane planned to make her move and see what the birthday boy had in his slacks that got Ms. China's nose wide open.

She doesn't even know how to tame him, Jane thought as she watched China and Smooth on the dance floor. *Everyone is getting their party on, and the Cîroc hasn't hit China yet.*

But when it does, I plan to snatch birthday boy away. If not tonight, I'll get my day with him! Jane thought.

Jane looked at Roxy and her new boyfriend, Sue Rabbit, who were having a splendid time. Roxy was backing her big booty onto Sue when Juvenile's "Back that Ass Up" came on.

Go ahead, Roxy! Jane thought as she began to groove with the music.

* * *

China and Smooth were getting their groove on to Juvenile. When China bent over, she felt Smooth's erection bulging. When she turned around to face him, she grabbed his hard cock.

"Hold your horses, baby! The night is still young, daddy!" China screamed.

She took a sip of her champagne, kissed Smooth, and passed the champagne into his mouth. Smooth swallowed it and then kissed China deeply.

"Happy birthday!"

"You've told me that all day!"

"That's how it's supposed to be!" China shouted.

All day, China had been showering Smooth with costly gifts, beginning with a delicious breakfast at an expensive restaurant. She had already spent over $50,000 spoiling Smooth with clothes, cologne, shoes, and jewelry. Even the twelve-layer chocolate cake sitting in VIP cost $5,000. GaGa had given Smooth a couple of church suits and made him promise that he would find a church one day and go for the Lord.

"Baby, I'ma having a ball already!"

Smooth stopped short when the big-ass bouncer whispered in his ear, "Mac needs to see you. It's urgent!"

The look on Smooth's face made China question, "What's wrong?"

"Mac wants to see me. I'll be back."

"No, Smooth! You're not gonna leave me out here by myself. I'm coming with you," China argued as she strutted off intertwined with him.

Heads turned as they walked off, as everyone couldn't help stare at China's jiggling ass in her skin-tight minidress and five-inch stilettos. Smooth was ready to get his groove on with China tonight.

Once they arrived in the office, Mac was sitting at his desk with his hands clamped together.

"Welcome, Smooth and China."

"Hey there, Mac. How's everything going? Your bouncer said that it was urgent. Is everything good?"

"Not necessarily, Smooth. We have a slight problem, and I don't know 'bout you, but I hate people who are out to ruin a good time. So I'ma see what your take is on people who want to fuck up a good time!" Mac said.

"Enlighten me."

"I will, Smooth. Follow me," Mac said as he led Smooth and China to his camera room. Once they were inside, Mac revealed to them the man who wanted Smooth dead.

* * *

"Esé, look at this señorita bonita," Joker said while showing Pascal an Instagram picture of a swimsuit model.

"Yeah, she's bad!" Pascal replied lustfully.

"Watch this. She's—"

Smash!

"What the fuck!" Pascal screamed, startled by the window shattering behind his head.

He was so focused on the front door that he left his backside unprotected. When he turned his face, he was staring down the barrel of Smooth's Glock .40. Joker slowly tried to raise his sniper rifle, but he never made it.

Boom! Boom!

"What the?" Pascal screamed as he turned toward the shots.

When he saw Joker's brains splattered on the dashboard and windshield, he vomited. Despite seeing death and dealing with death in Miami, Pascal wasn't ready to stomach his own death.

"Who sent you, esé?" China asked, appearing in the passenger window with a Glock .50 aimed at him.

"Please lie to us!" Smooth said, ramming his Glock against the back of Pascal's head.

Fuck it! I'ma gonna die anyway, he thought.

"One more time, esé! Who sent you?" Smooth asked.

"You're a dead man, Smooth. The streets will always be M-13's."

Boom! Boom! Boom! Boom!

China squeezed first, and Smooth joined her. Together, they emptied their clips into Pascal and then walked away from the SUV.

"I still have one more present for you, baby," China said as they walked back into the club as if nothing had happened.

"Y'all keep sneaking off and getting y'all groove on, and I'ma throw cake in y'all's faces," Roxy said as she walked up with Sue Rabbit holding onto her waist from behind.

"Birthday shout out to Smooth!" the DJ announced over the mic.

"You're famous, daddy!" China said.

"Yeah, that means you are too."

"Oh, is that right?"

"I could never be wrong about my equal!" Smooth shouted.

"I love you, daddy!"

"And I love you, too."

"Another hour and we're out!" China said over Yo Gotti's "Down in the DM."

"Okay," Smooth said as he took China into his arms and kissed her passionately.

"Thank you for having my back."

"I'll never leave you stranded, Smooth. You know that!" China said, immediately having a flash of Tracy before her eyes.

* * *

"Yo, this muthafucka's not picking up. Neither him or Joker, esé," Mario said to Juan.

"Maybe they can't pick up right now. He might have the Negro in the scope right now, homes," Juan replied.

"Yeah, that's true."

"Tomorrow we get the one hundred kilos. With him dead, the tail will die," Juan explained. "After we do get rid of these Negros, we will make their workers make up their minds. Death or work for the M-13s," he continued.

"That sounds like a plan, esé!" Mario said as he bit into a McDonald's Big Mac.

Juan grabbed his phone off the living room glass table as it rang.

"Hola?"

"Pascal and Joker are dead," Javier said to Juan, causing him to sit up straight.

"Get the fuck out of here!"

"I'm serious on M-13's *vida*! They're dead."

"The Negro is too smart for death," Juan replied. He couldn't believe his ears. *How could it be so?* he wanted to know. "Who's giving you this info?"

"Felix found them," Javier said, speaking of one of the bouncers working at Club Rage who had no connection to Mac other than a paycheck.

"Fuck!" Juan screamed as he hung up his phone.

"What's wrong, esé?" Mario asked a frustrated Juan.

"Pascal and Joker are dead."

* * *

Smooth and China retired to a rental beach house on South Beach. Lying in bed blindfolded, Smooth allowed

China to take control. She kissed his lips as she straddled him, and then she trailed her tongue down his neck to his nipples.

"I love you, Smooth. Remember, I would do anything for you. I would share the world with you, daddy," China whispered in his ear as she resumed kissing him.

"I love you too, China, and I will always be here for us, baby."

Smooth stopped speaking when he felt hands wrap around his cock and a warm mouth take his erection to bliss. He knew it wasn't China, because he could still feel her lips brushing up against his.

"Happy birthday, baby. It's too much fun not to share it three ways, daddy," China said as Tracy slowly sucked Smooth's dick. China removed the blindfold and then stared into Smooth's eyes. China kissed him again and then stepped aside to let him see Tracy.

When Smooth looked down, his heart dropped, and he was hit with an extreme guilt trip.

She wasn't hiding shit from me. She was preparing this all along, he realized.

Smooth was staring at the same beautiful redbone chic that China was captured kissing in the parking lot.

"Meet Tracy. Tracy, meet my man, Smooth."

Tracy lifted her head and stroked Smooth's cock as she spoke.

"Happy birthday, Smooth."

The threesome had a splendid time. China had opened a door to their relationship that they had tried to pursue with

Rebecca. However, Smooth had no clue that the devil was sucking his dick and sharing the same woman with him. Tracy demanded that Smooth fuck her in her ass while she ate China's pussy.

Now this is what you call heaven! Smooth thought as he penetrated Tracy deeply and unmercifully.

"Yes! Mmmmm," Tracy shouted.

"Uhhh shit! I'm coming!" China purred loudly as she squirted cum all in Tracy's face.

12

"Yo, Banga! What's up?" Adam asked him as he pulled up to the corner store.

"You tell me, lil nigga! What's the play?"

"We need more product. Me and Jess making a super killing."

"How much you need?" Banga asked.

"I need at least fourteen ounces. I'ma be able to get rid of seven of them in the next hour."

"Damn, lil nigga! You really making numbers flip, huh?"

"Wait until school starts back," Adam added.

"Listen! I'ma go get that shit ready for you. Come see me in an hour, and I mean an hour, not all day," Banga informed Adam.

"Okay."

"Yo, Banga, let me holla at you," a hustler named Var called on Banga after coming out of Jake's corner store.

"Yellow!"

"Man, I need some help out here. I holla'd at Ham, and he told me to get up with you when I seen you," Var said.

"So Ham ain't have it to help you out, bro?" Banga asked.

"Man, Ham eating everything out here. The shit he cutting up looks like Kibbles & Bits!" Var explained.

"Damn Ham short-stopping the block." Banga couldn't tell the difference being that he no longer was out hustling on the block. Banga was now the man in Martin Count regulating all the hoods. He had competition in the Hobe Sound area beefing with him and had plans to get rid of him. This is something Banga did not tell Smooth, who he knew would come from Miami and help him if he called on him.

"Var, listen! What is it that you want to do?"

"Man, I need half a brick, Banga. You know I'ma get that money out here."

"I got you. Just give me an hour. We go back, Var, so I know you good. I'ma have a talk with Ham as soon as I see him," Banga said.

"Thank you, bro. I know you'll help me out," Var answered.

After going inside the corner store and purchasing a six-pack of Budweiser, Banga went back to the trap house on 8th Street to prepare all the orders that his clientele requested. When he got done wrapping up everything, he saw that he was getting low on product.

Damn, I need to re-up! Banga thought as he pulled out his iPhone to call Smooth.

"What's up, Yellow?" Smooth answered on the second ring.

"Man, what's good? I need to see you."

"Damn, Banga. I just left you."

"Money that fast, my nigga. How you looking?" Banga asked.

"Come see me. I'm still good up here. What is it you need?"

"I need another twenty, bro."

"I got you. Come through. Sue Rabbit will have everything ready for you."

"Alright, my nigga. I'm coming tonight," Banga replied.

"Got you," Smooth said as he disconnected the call.

* * *

Tina raised out of bed when she heard Ham step out to go hustle. It was 8:00 p.m., and he wouldn't be home until 10:00 p.m. She walked into the bathroom and went to her secret hiding spot underneath the sink. She retrieved a small pouch the size of a small wallet, sat on the toilet, and then unzipped it. She pulled out her lighter and crack pipe. In a small baggie, Tina had crack that she had stolen from Ham.

If he catches me, he will kill me! Tina thought as she placed the crack in her pipe and then put flame to it.

Tina inhaled the crack smoke, held it in for thirty seconds, and then exhaled and immediately felt the intense high. Tina was seriously battling her resurfaced crack addiction. She thought she had the power to leave it alone, but recently she returned to her habit, hiding it from Ham. She knew the risk she was putting the baby in, but she just couldn't help it. Crack was her friend and the only thing that kept her calm.

Lord, please protect my baby! she thought as she replaced her pouch and returned to bed, where she slept peacefully.

* * *

"Yo! The feds are everywhere. They're driving in unmarked sedans and sports cars, so be careful," Smooth warned his coworkers in the trap house.

After learning from Guru's girl, Landi, that Metro-Dade detectives were moving to stop the drug war, Smooth called for an emergency meeting.

"Guru? Banga's coming through to pick up some product. Me and Sue Rabbit won't be here, so be on point. Big Mitch, keep your eyes open. We don't know how they're coming, and like these Mexicans, they're enemies too. So they'll get it as well," Smooth explained.

"Do you mind me asking a question?" Big Mitch inquired.

"Go ahead, Mitch," Smooth permitted.

"Wouldn't you think for safe purposes that while they are hot and on the prowl, that we slow down and close up shop until they hit dead end?"

"It's wise, Mitch, but we are about our money and not being afraid of the police. Thanks to our brother, Guru, we have inside connections infiltrating the department. So we will always know their movement. Miami is our streets, and the war with these Mexicans will not rest until we make them bow down. We are the kings of the streets, not these wetbacks," Smooth explained, looking into the eyes of thirty of his main men. "We lose one and gain three by nightfall."

"I got you, boss," Mitch said, nodding his head up and down in agreement with his superior.

"This meeting is over. Everyone dismissed! Mall, stay behind. I need to have a word with you," Smooth said.

After everyone filed out, one behind the other, Sue Rabbit walked up to Mall and squeezed his shoulders while looking him in his eyes. "You're a good man, and I want you to know that. I'ma tell you something, and I want you to understand me clearly," Sue Rabbit began, still staring seriously into his eyes.

"I got you, bro. Always," Mall answered as he looked over at Smooth.

"Thirty men stood here for an hour and listened to Smooth talk. How many do you think understood him like you understood him?" Sue Rabbit asked.

The question perplexed Mall because he wasn't sure where Sue Rabbit was heading.

"I'm guessing everyone understood, being that they were even under this roof," Mall answered.

Sue Rabbit then smiled.

"That's why I'm proud of you, Mall. You know the men like you know the block," Smooth said, stepping up to him and standing next to Sue.

"I'm making you a lieutenant, Mall. I want you to thread out all the weak links in our hood and our traps. The feds don't stop shit, and by all means, we plan to prove it," Smooth added.

"I got you, boss," Mall replied.

* * *

When Smooth came through the door, Zorro attacked him, jumping up and down, and the good smell of soul food was redolently lingering in the atmosphere of the apartment. "Honey, I'm home!"

"I'm in the kitchen, baby!" China shouted back.

When Smooth walked into the kitchen, he found China and GaGa sitting at the table. He hugged GaGa and kissed her on her cheek, and then he hugged and kissed China.

"Hey, ma!"

"Smooth, how are you doing, son?"

"I'm okay, ma."

"That's so good. I just stopped by to see if you've worn any of them suits to someone's church yet," GaGa said.

"You know what, ma?"

"What?" GaGa said, putting her hands on her hips with a pout on her face.

Like mother, like daughter, Smooth thought.

"I was going to find some time this weekend, ma."

"Well, that's good. Make sure I get the pictures, okay?"

"Yes, ma'am," Smooth replied.

"So tell me, what are y'all cooking in here, China?" Smooth asked as he walked to the stove and reached for a pot lid, until China slapped him on his hand.

"That's a big no-no!"

"What?" Smooth asked.

"Go wash your hands, and I'll fix you a plate. Then you'll see what's in the pots," China requested.

"Okay. You got that!"

"No, y'all got that!" GaGa said, backing up China.

Smooth raised his hands in surrender. "I don't want no trouble," he said as he strutted off to wash his hands.

Before he made it to the bathroom, Zorro began barking at someone knocking at the door.

Woof! Woof! Woof!

"Who the hell is that?" Smooth said out loud as he about-faced and walked toward the front door. "I got it, China!"

"Zorro, shut up, boy!" Smooth shouted to the dog, who obeyed and sat down.

When Smooth looked through the peephole, he saw Tracy's fine ass in her work clothes.

Damn! This bitch is gorgeous! Smooth thought as he opened the door.

"Hey, baby girl," Smooth said as he hugged Tracy.

"How are you? Damn! It smells good in here!"

"That's China and GaGa," Smooth informed her.

"GaGa's here?" Tracy said excitedly as she quickly walked into the kitchen and hugged the two women.

Damn! One big happy family! Smooth thought.

Together the threesome ate dinner and chatted over wine until GaGa left to go home.

After they cleaned up, the trio moved to the bedroom.

"That's a good meal y'all put together," Smooth said to China, who was in bed straddling him while Tracy lay next to them.

"I'm full, but I still got it in me to make you happy, daddy. Ain't that right, Tracy?"

"Yes, baby. We could make daddy happy," Tracy replied as she began planting soft kisses from Smooth's chest to his cock, which was already bulging through his Polo briefs.

Tracy pulled out his cock and stuck it in her mouth.

"Mmmm!" she moaned as she slowly and deeply sucked his dick.

China straddled Smooth and kissed him passionately. She then climbed off him and positioned herself behind Tracy, who put her ass up in the air while she continued to suck Smooth's dick. China spread Tracy's ass cheeks and stuck her tongue inside, causing Tracy to let out a soft moan.

China badly wanted to put on a strap-on, but that was something that only she and Tracy did together. China ate Tracy's pussy from the back until she came to an electrifying orgasm. China wanted to feel Smooth inside her, so she pushed Tracy up to Smooth's face, which she straddled while he ate her pussy. China then got in a reverse cowgirl position and slid down onto Smooth's hard cock.

"Yes, daddy!" China purred as she began to ride him slowly.

* * *

Two of Smooth's soldiers had pulled up to McDonald's and seen the three M-13 Mexicans inside standing in line.

"Bro! Fuck it! We ought to hit up their ass now. Shit! If

98

it was us, they'd done squeezed, my nigga!" said Smoky, a sixteen-year-old straight hothead.

His homeboy Killa was eighteen years old and was the smart one. However, most times, he was influenced easily by Smoky.

"Well, we'll wait until they come out, bro, and light up their asses!" Killa suggested.

"Yeah!" Smoky said, racking his AK-47.

It was five minutes later when the M-13s started to make their exit.

"Let's run this shit!"

"Po-po!" Killa screamed, trying to stop Smoky, who had already hopped out of the Chevy that Killa was driving.

Chop! Chop! Chop! Chop!

"Police!" Killa screamed, but he couldn't get Smoky's attention.

Smoky hit all three of the Mexicans, but he never saw the unmarked Yukon SUV until the lights came on.

"Freeze! Put down your weapon!"

Chop! Chop! Chop! Chop!

Before the detective could fire, Killa backed himself and Smoky into cover. Smoky was then able to jump back inside the Chevy while the detectives fired at the car as Killa backed out.

Boc! Boc! Boc! Boc!

Killa was fortunate that he was in a good angle to avoid the bullets coming through the Chevy's doors and window; however, Smoky was not. He was hit in his neck and chest, and trying to hold on to what was left of life.

"Fuck, man! I told you police, my nigga!" Killa screamed as he gave chase.

The detectives hopped behind him and had backup coming from all angles.

"Damn it!" Killa exclaimed when he looked over at Smoky and saw the stagnant stare in his eyes.

Smoky was dead, and now Killa was alone taking Metro-Dade on a wild chase.

"I can't go back to jail, my nigga! Why you got to be such a hothead, Smoky?"

Smack!

Killa slapped a dead Smoky as he artistically navigated the Chevy. But dozens of Metro-Dade police were chasing him at ninety miles per hour. He turned on 169th, making a sharp right, and fled through road spikes.

"Damn!" Killa exclaimed as the tires went flat and sparks went wild.

A helicopter came and flooded the darkness with its spotlight.

"Fuck, Smoky. Why?" Killa asked a dead Smoky, who was laid out in the passenger seat. Killa turned right on 173rd and quickly hopped out on his feet and ran for it.

Boc! Boc! Boc! Boc! Boc!

Metro-Dade wasn't taking any chances. They gunned down Killa, filling his body with a storm of bullets. He was dead before he hit the ground.

13

*M*iranda had called Smooth and informed him of the nice baby mansion she had in Miami Gardens. He and China wasted no time getting over to see the beautiful home.

"This place is marvelous!" China exclaimed excitedly while adoring the master bedroom. "This place is beautiful, baby. It's so big!" China gushed as she walked further into the room that had a view of the city.

The mansion was a five-bedroom palace that sat on 7,390 square feet. It had its own wine room and a unique swimming pool. Miranda gave them a tour of the entire house, both upstairs and downstairs.

She just knew that Smooth would buy the house and that he would love it. She was hoping to catch Smooth by himself, but he had brought China along. As Miranda watched China melt, she felt jealousy creeping into her mind. She once wanted Smooth for herself, but he had chosen to stay with China.

"So, Miranda, how much is the owner wanting?" Smooth asked.

"The owner is asking $2.3 million."

"What? $2.3 million? Smooth, no way will this be a straight target!" China said.

"China, let me handle this, okay?"

"Whatever!" China said, catching his attitude.

His mind to buy the home was already made up the moment he had seen China's acceptance when she walked through the door. Smooth ignored her attitude and then turned back to Miranda.

"How much lower can you get it?"

"Smooth, the original price was," Miranda began as she opened the folder and flipped through a couple pages, "$3.8 million. Being that they want a fast sale of the house, the agency dropped it to 2.3," Miranda explained.

"Damn! So there's no way around the 2.3, huh?"

Yeah! Some dick! Miranda wanted to say. "If there is, I'll have to check with my superiors," she said instead.

Smooth thought for a moment. He had $2.3 million put up, and he really wanted to get the house for him, China, and Tracy. China insisted that they would be targets, but Smooth didn't give two shits about the police.

"Give me two days, and I'll have the $2.3 million for you, Miranda. Just don't let no one buy the house before I get the money to you," he told her.

"Okay, the house is on hold," Miranda replied and then wrote a side note in the folder.

The ill look on China's face revealed her disappointment. As they were heading back to the car, Smooth's iPhone chimed with Yo Gotti's ring tone.

"Hello?" he answered.

"Hey, mon, me need to see you, mon!" Stone said.

"What's good?"

"Me need twenty."

"I got you. I'ma stop by later tonight. Is that good?" Smooth asked.

"Yeah, mon! See you tonight, mon," Stone replied before hanging up.

Damn! I need to hit Amanda up and get some shit cooked up, Smooth thought as he got inside his truck with an uptight China.

"What the fuck is yo problem? You were just all gleeful, and all of a sudden, you acting like a damn sour ball?" Smooth asked China, who simply stared out the window.

"You think you have everything figured out, Smooth!" China exploded.

"And what do you mean by that?"

"Why would you come out of your pockets with $2.3 million for a house? What job do you have to account for the money, huh? What career do you have, Smooth? Come on, man. Be smart!" China shouted angrily.

What she was saying was some real shit, but Smooth wasn't trying to hear that.

"China, listen. Do you think I give a fuck about the police, huh?" Smooth yelled.

"Oh, so you don't care about hurting the people you love?" she asked.

"I didn't say that. Don't be putting words in my mouth."

"So what are you saying, Smooth?" China asked, staring daggers at him as he drove through traffic.

"What I'm saying is I'm not worried."

"Fuck you, Smooth! Do what the fuck you want to do! If you want to be out here risking your fucking freedom when you have niggas to do it, then be a hard-ass who has everything figured out!" she told him before turning up the volume on the radio.

Smooth let China have the battle he was having with her, but she would never understand the love and loyalty he had for the empire he had built. Sue Rabbit and Guru could handle things by themselves, but he wouldn't leave them on the front line by themselves. Smooth loved China to death, and he understood her worry for him, but he was always watching out before he stepped outside. He also always checked his rear-view mirror for Juan José and Mario Lopez.

I've come too far escaping death to let these Mexicans lay me down. I refuse to hide like a little bitch! Smooth thought.

* * *

Roxy took the day off from the restaurant and let her assistant manager, Nicole, keep things running. She was spending time with Sue Rabbit, who she had become close with, and she loved the affection with which he showered her. On the other hand, Sue had been turning down his sideline bitches and dedicating all his time to her.

"Sitting on the beach having a picnic while bathing in the sun, Sue Rabbit caressed Roxy's thighs as she straddled him. She wore a sun hat and sunglasses. Although she had shades covering her eyes, Sue Rabbit could still see the passion she had for him.

"Trayvon?" Roxy called Sue Rabbit by his first name, a name she loved calling him more so than his street name.

"What's up, beautiful?" Sue Rabbit answered.

"Where do you see this going with us?"

"I thought you'd never ask."

"Why?" Roxy replied.

"Because, sometimes it's good to let love be love."

"Is that what you call this?" Roxy asked.

With his hands behind his head while Roxy caressed his eight-pack, Sue Rabbit propped up on his elbows, removed her shades, and looked deep into her eyes.

"I call this two people who want the same thing and who have found a steady heartbeat. Roxy, I'ma be real with you. It's no secret that I'm out here in these streets. It's not forever. I have my limits. I used to associate with other women, but since being with you, it's ceased. Baby, it's only ceased because I have what I want in my life."

"And what is that, Trayvon?"

"You are beautiful! All of you," Sue said to Roxy, causing her smile with joy, fulfilled on the inside.

She leaned over and kissed Sue passionately, not caring who was looking.

"Just don't hurt me, Trayvon. I'm a real woman who will be your backbone through whatever. But the moment you hurt me, you think China could be a bitch sometimes. I'm her big sister, so guess where she gets it from?" Roxy explained.

"Let's see if you can back up what you're saying in the room," he said.

"Okay," Roxy replied as she stood up and bent over to grab the picnic basket.

Sue stared at her ass and pussy bulging through her bikini.

"Damn!" Sue Rabbit exclaimed loud enough for Roxy to hear the lust in his voice.

Roxy turned around and caught Sue Rabbit checking her out. She knew she had a nice body, and that she had Sue Rabbit's head all fucked up.

"Come on, Trayvon. Before I change my mind."

"I'll still wait on you to change your mind again, baby," Sue said as he stood up and grabbed a handful of Roxy's ass.

Back at the room, Sue Rabbit made love to Roxy like she was the last woman on the face of the earth. It had been a long time since Roxy had not been treated with the same affection that she got from Sue. She just knew that she had found the man of her dreams. He was different from every man she had been with, and especially different from the other men in Miami.

* * *

Mall had made his cousin Choppa his sergeant and right-hand man. They were holding down the block and being careful to avoid the feds, who were riding through the hoods boldly trying to find weak links. Mall and Choppa were tired of the feds snooping.

"Man, that cracker just gonna sit there all day, bro? We ain't gonna be able to make no money," Choppa said to Mall.

Every crackhead driving through 112th saw the feds and kept driving. They didn't want to risk stopping and buying drugs. Mall was the lieutenant and knew that it would look bad if he didn't put a handle on the situation. They were losing money by letting the feds stick around. Mall looked at his Rolex and saw that it was 5:45 p.m. In another fifteen minutes, the sun would be going down.

"Let's wait until the sun goes down," Mall told Choppa.

"You serious?"

"Since when I ever tell you something that I don't do?" Mall replied as he walked away toward the trap house.

When Mall went inside the trap house, he called Sue Rabbit on his phone.

"Hello."

"Yo, bro, this Mall."

"What's good, Mall?" Sue Rabbit asked, still in bed with Roxy at their hotel.

"We have problems on 112th, bro."

"Talk to me," Sue prodded.

"Feds been on the block all day, and money being passed up. Too many are scared to even stop and get served."

"What, they just sitting there plain as day?"

"Exactly," Mall replied.

"Damn! How much money have you made today?"

"None, other than the neighborhood," Mall informed Sue Rabbit.

"So what's on your mind, Mall. Are you wanting to shut down shop?"

"If we shut down shop, we're only preparing ourselves to see it tomorrow. I want to handle this one, Sue Rabbit," Mall expressed.

Sue knew exactly what Mall meant by handling this one, and he thought about the potential heat that might follow.

Fuck it! Shit! One fall and they'll back out and not sit on a nigga's block fucking up money. It's a war on drugs, and they are the enemies too! Sue Rabbit thought.

"Be careful, soldier. And make sure you get 'em!" Sue Rabbit gave Mall the green light.

"I will, bro," Mall said as he hung up.

* * *

After dropping off China, Smooth then picked up Amanda in his Range Rover to take her to the new trap where she'd cook up the product. Monica was playing on the radio, and Amanda could tell that something was bothering Smooth. She reached out and turned down the radio volume.

"What's wrong?"

Smooth looked at Amanda and then back at the road.

"Why do you feel like something is wrong?"

"Because I know you more than you think I do."

Smooth sighed and then spoke.

"The woman I try so hard to please is always trying to make me retire from the game. I got too much shit I've built to let go and leave my niggas alone," Smooth explained.

Amanda unfastened her seat belt and slid over near Smooth. She kissed him on his cheek and then whispered in his ear.

"When number one fails, number two will carry you."

Smooth looked over at Amanda and then pecked her on her lips.

"I hear you," he said.

As much as he didn't want to fuck other women behind China's back, the temptation was too great for Smooth.

And Amanda is too damn beautiful, Smooth thought.

"You miss me?" Smooth said to Amanda, who was massaging the back of his neck.

"Yes, I miss you, Smooth," she said as he was pulling inside the apartment complex.

"Let's get inside," Smooth said as he killed the engine.

"Okay."

"I want to see how much you really miss me, baby," Smooth said as he kissed Amanda on her sexy lips.

Together they stepped out of the Range Rover and walked inside the apartment, both unaware of the eyes watching them from another apartment.

* * *

"Choppa, I want you and Money to take them from the left side. Just position yourself in Ms. Pearl's yard and wait until you hear the first round, bro," Mall told his sergeant.

"I got you, bro!" Choppa replied.

"Y'all niggas ready for this shit?"

"Born ready," Money said.

"Well, let's get this shit done, so we can get back to getting this money, my niggas!"

Mall waited until Choppa and Money walked over to the next block and then came back to 112th through backyards, until they were in Ms. Pearl's yard.

Mall waited until the crackhead walked up to the feds' unmarked car to do the task he was paid to do.

"Hey, police, we need your help. There's a kid dying on the sidewalk. He just got stabbed, man. Don't let the kid die!" the crackhead told the two federal agents, who were hesitant to let down their window.

The muscular FBI agent who was driving rolled down the window.

"What's the problem, old man? Are you high or drunk?"

"Man, I'm telling you, a kid is dying behind that building over there," the crackhead pointed. "Please help him. He's my nephew."

"Let's go check this out, Thomas," the agent told his partner.

"2052 respond to 112th," the agent said into the radio.

Just as the agent took two steps out of the sedan, a bullet exploded his head and dropped him to his death. His partner immediately hid for cover on the passenger side, looking for the shooter. Before he could radio that an officer was down, Choppa pulled the trigger to his AK-15 and took out Agent Thomas from behind in Ms. Pearl's yard.

"I bet that'll keep y'all out of the hood," Mall said as he ran back inside the trap house.

Choppa ran up to the crackhead and shot him twice in the head.

"No witnesses. Sorry!" Choppa said to the dead man before running to the trap house as well.

Money waited until the backup arrived. They then took the two agents by surprise, nailing them as they stepped out of their unmarked sedan.

Chop! Chop! Chop!

"How 'bout that backup. Officer down!" Money screamed and then fled the area.

14

Jane was off the clock that day, and her kids were in Orlando with her mother for the weekend. When she saw Smooth pull up with the beautiful woman who was never home, she became a little jealous. All types of speculations ran through her mind about Smooth and her neighbor. She wanted to be in Smooth's presence right then. In nothing but her T-shirt and panties, Jane thought of a plan. She picked up her cell phone while sitting on the sofa and staring outside, focused on her neighbor's front door. She called China, who picked up the phone on the first ring.

"Hello?"

"Hey, girl, this Jane."

"I know how to read caller ID," China replied. "What's up?"

"I'm just curious. I have plumbing problems. How do I get a hold of the landlord? I'm getting the neighbor's shit filling up my toilet every time they use theirs."

"I will have him call you. Give me a second, okay?" China said as she put Jane on hold.

* * *

"Mmmm, Smooth!" Amanda purred as Smooth fucked her hard from the back on the living room sofa.

Smooth was taking out all his frustration from China, on Amanda.

I just want to keep her happy, and yet she can't let go of trying to determine how to run my shit! he thought.

"Baby, I'm coming!" Amanda moaned out loud as her body began to tremble.

"Arggghh, shit!" Smooth groaned, exploding inside Amanda's pussy.

She worked her pussy muscles skillfully and gripped Smooth's cock.

"Damn!" Smooth exclaimed.

"Damn what?" she asked while tightly squeezing his dick with her pussy.

"You're amazing, baby!" Smooth said as he pulled out and sat down on the sofa with his pants around his ankles, too exhausted to pull them up.

Smooth watched as Amanda stood up and walked into the bathroom.

Who the hell is calling me? Smooth thought, feeling the vibration of his iPhone in his pants around his ankles.

He dug into his pockets and retrieved his phone. Seeing that it was China, he answered. "What's up?" he said dryly.

"Don't play with me, Smooth. You can have an attitude all you want to."

"Oh my gosh, China. What is it?" Smooth exclaimed.

"Fuck you, dumbass! You have plumbing problems in your apartment complex. Could you please go see how a good landlord could fix the problem?" China asked.

"Who is it?"

"My girl, Jane."

The bitch who's always giving me the bedroom eyes, he thought.

"Could you please go check her out? She's home and off work today. You'll go, right?" China said.

Smooth sighed loud enough for China to hear.

"Back to you, too," China said, "but that don't answer my question."

"I'll go. See you later. Love you," Smooth said.

"Love you and hate you too," China replied, and then hung up the phone.

Smooth pulled up his pants and then walked into the bathroom where Amanda was stepping out of the shower.

"I gotta go see about one of the apartments. Start cooking so I can handle business, okay?"

"I'm on it, baby," Amanda said as she dried her hair with the towel that she just had wrapped around her nude body.

"Let me go before you make me change my mind," Smooth said as he strutted out of the bathroom and the apartment altogether.

* * *

"What do you think about it?" China asked Tracy, who she had just told about Smooth's ridiculous decision to buy a $2.3 million home.

Tracy was at work and just about to get off.

"I think we should just move in and try to protect him, China. He's too much in the street, and there's nothing no woman can do to change a street nigga."

"I just don't want nothing bad to happen to him. It'll hurt me to lose him to the stupidity. He cares too much for his homeboys, and that shit really irks me."

Who is calling me? China thought while looking at her phone.

"Hold on, Tracy. Someone's calling me," China said as she clicked over to answer the incoming call.

"Hello."

"This is a collect call from Jenny Davis, an inmate at Lowell Correctional Institution. If you want to accept the call, press zero."

China pressed zero.

"This call may be recorded and monitored. Thank you for using GTL," the automated voice said before connecting the call.

"What's up, baby?" Jenny's voice boomed through the phone.

"I'm okay. What about you, baby?" China replied.

"I'm missing you. Did you get my letter and pictures?"

"Yeah, I got them. Hold on a sec. I have someone on the other line," China informed her.

"Okay."

Click!

"Tracy?"

"Yeah."

"I'll be waiting on you. I have to take this call."

"Okay, I'll be getting off shortly," Tracy said as she hung up.

Click!

"Jenny?"

"Yeah, I'm here. What's good?"

"I'm good, although things are up with Smooth again. It's just selfish how he won't let these streets go!" China explained to Jenny.

"What happened now?" she asked.

"Why would a man with no job go and purchase a $2.3 million home when the feds are cracking down?"

"Sounds like someone don't believe that their shit stinks!" Jenny replied.

"Like he tells it, it's fuck the police!"

"That sounds a lot like a careless soul. What about the ones who love him?"

"I brought that up, and he still remains nonchalant. I'm tired of worrying if he will come home at night. It's beginning to get too exhausting, Jenny," China said.

"Don't let it run you crazy, baby. Try to show him the hard way until he gets the picture."

"And what is that, baby?"

"You have one minute remaining," the automated voice chimed in.

"Leave him until he chooses the right decision," Jenny suggested.

"Make him choose?"

"Exactly."

"I love you, Jenny."

"I love you too."

"Thank you for using GTL," the automated voice said before disconnecting the call.

"Damn it! I hate that damn shit!" China exclaimed, wishing they had more time.

China then thought seriously about what Jenny had suggested.

Leave him until he gets the picture, China thought in retrospection of Jenny's advice. *Could I really live without him? Of course you can, girl. You have Tracy, and she has you!* China's inner voice screamed at her. *I'ma see what he really loves first, money or me!* she thought as she sat on the sofa flipping through channels.

When she got to BET, she saw Beyoncé's new hit playing.

Damn, that's a bad bitch that nigga Jay-Z got! China thought, getting wet between her legs for Beyoncé.

* * *

When Jane heard the knocks at the door, she ran and looked through her peephole.

"Oh my gosh! It's him!" Jane exclaimed in a whisper.

She looked at herself indecisively, wondering whether she should throw on some pants. She was still in her T-shirt and panties.

Fuck that. I'm take this dick! she thought as she slid off her black thong and tossed it onto the sofa. She was already wet just thinking of how good he would fuck her.

Jane then opened the door and stared at Smooth in his eyes. *Damn!* she thought, lusting over his handsomeness.

Smooth himself was speechless as he stared back at Jane, who was a beautiful redbone dime piece at five three and 125 pounds.

"Ummm, I got a call, from uh . . ."

"China called you about my plumbing," Jane helped Smooth.

"Yeah, I'm the landlord. Can I take a look?"

"Yes, come in and close the door," Jane said as she spun on her heels.

Smooth looked at the hump raising Jane's T-shirt over her ass, and instantly became erect, staring at her red cheeks and her moist thong on the sofa.

If this isn't a booty call, what the hell is it? Smooth thought as he closed the front door and followed Jane into the apartment.

When Smooth entered the bathroom, he was slapped in the face by the view of Jane's phat pussy as she bent over to lift up the toilet seat.

"I think I need a plunger. What do you think?" Jane asked Smooth while looking back at him and spreading her pussy lips apart, revealing a wet tunnel. "I promise, China will never find out, Smooth. I just want you to fuck the shit out of me!" she said seductively.

With no words needed to be spoken, Smooth unfastened his belt and pulled out his dick. Smooth then walked up to Jane, grabbed her by her small waist, and plunged his cock deep into her graveyard.

"Oh my gosh, you're huge!" Jane moaned out in a gasp. Jane was in heaven as Smooth fucked the shit out of her, and had yet another victim on her hands and under her belt.

* * *

"Damn! That is crazy! You guys really serious, huh?" Landi asked Guru, who was lying behind her cozily on the sofa watching the breaking news.

The shooting that occurred on 112th went national and had the president of the United States highly upset.

"You do know they're about to come down hard on your people, Guru, right?" Landi asked while looking over her shoulder.

"Hey, shit happens!" Guru replied, kissing her on her cheek.

"Promise me that you'll give it up soon."

"I told you, as soon as Juan takes his last breath, I'm out. I just can't leave my boys in the middle of a war."

Guru explained the situation to Landi, who understood the love he had for his crew. Just the previous week, Guru had comforted Landi, who had spilled her desire to keep him in her life. She cried in his arms and begged for him to let the street life go, but to keep the bad-boy attitude. It was a moment of laughter and contentedness that resulted in them making love that night.

"I understand what you mean, baby. Shit, if I could help you find him tonight, I would," Landi told Guru as she flipped the channel to a Latino station where Jennifer Lopez was performing onstage live in concert.

"You know, I took a picture with her in my freshman year of high school," Landi said.

"Really?"

"Yeah, I bet you'll love that, huh?"

"I think any man would love it, baby," Guru replied.

"Like every woman would love to take Usher to bed," Landi said.

"Are you in them statistics?"

"Nope!"

"You're lying, because it came out too damn fast."

"Whatever!" Landi said as she turned around and stared at Guru with her bedroom eyes. "The DEA is talking about doing a sweep on any man standing."

"Is this what your girl is telling you?" Guru asked.

"Yeah, she called me last night actually. They're moving to take down Juan, too, when they find him," she informed him.

"I don't think my boy would like the DEA taking down Juan before he could kill him."

"Well, your boy better hurry up and find him," Landi stated. "Because either grave or prison, you're out baby, right?"

"Yeah!" Guru said.

"Smart man!" Landi added.

* * *

The four Mexican teenagers were playing basketball at their community park. The court lights illuminated the court brightly, but not the darkened streets. When Spencer arrived, he sat down on the bleachers. The four boys were too engrossed in their game and never saw him sitting down watching the good game. Each time one scored, the other team responded. Spencer pulled out a silencer from his pants pocket and then screwed it onto his FN 5.7. Spencer set the pistol on his lap and then leaned back against the bleachers with his hands locked behind his head.

"Hurry, esé! Hurry!" one of the teens shouted for his partner to shoot the ball.

"So we have someone who speaks English out here," Spencer said.

His adrenaline began pumping rapidly. For the first time after all the slaughter he had been committing across Miami, someone finally spoke English.

This is great! Spencer thought as he continued to watch the game.

"Come on, esé, and shoot the damn ball!" the tall teen shouted to his partner.

For him to be talking English, that means all of them understand it well, Spencer reflected.

"Carlos, hurry man. Shake him!"

Spencer leaned up, looked around, and saw no witnesses around. He grabbed his FN 5.7 pistol and indecisively aimed at the court, swaying from boy to boy. When the tall teen went up for a layup, Spencer pulled the trigger three times, exploding the teen's head.

"Oh shit, Carlos! What the fuck!" one of the teens screamed, with blood from his friend's head all over his face and clothes.

Everyone looked around in fear in search of the shooter. Spencer began clapping his hands to reveal his location. The three teens were extremely shaken up, and they stuck in their tracks like deer trapped in the headlights.

"Homes, run!" one of the boys yelled as he took off.

He didn't get very far, as Spencer shot him in the leg from the court, knocking him down.

"You want to run, eh?" Spencer addressed the boy who he had just shot.

The other two looked at Spencer, afraid to blink the wrong way.

"Esé, run!" the boy encouraged the two remaining.

Spencer looked at the two scared boys and aimed at the boy on the ground while looking at the other two again. He then pulled the trigger.

Psst! Psst! Psst! Psst!

"I dare you two to try and run. I promise that you'll end up the same way," Spencer warned the boys after killing the boy on the ground.

"Now, I'ma ask you guys this one time. Where do I find Juan and Mario?"

"Two blocks away at the Mexican joint."

* * *

After fucking Jane from the bathroom to the living room, Smooth walked back over to Amanda's and grabbed the product that she had already finished. He then left to deliver the product to Stone. Smooth honked the horn twice and then began removing the product from his stash spot. Stone came outside carrying a duffel bag of money and tossed it in the backseat of Smooth's SUV.

"Hey, mon, everything is there," Stone said as he came around to the driver's seat and grabbed the bag from Smooth.

"And like always, everything is there too," Smooth said as he hopped back into the driver's seat.

"Hey, mon, be careful. The police are everywhere. Someone killed four of them in your backyard. So be careful."

"What you mean in my backyard?" Smooth asked, confused.

"You didn't hear about the feds getting blasted on 112th? The shit is everywhere, mon. It's national."

"Hell no! I ain't hear shit like that. I'ma see you later, Stone. Call me when you need something else," Smooth said as he then pulled off, calling Sue Rabbit on his phone.

Sue Rabbit picked up on the third ring, sounding like he was just waking up.

It is only a little after 9:00. Why is he in bed instead of working? Smooth wanted to know.

"Sue, what the fuck is going on over on 112th?" Smooth exclaimed.

"Shit, four birds got popped. That's it!" Sue said.

"Who ordered it? People don't just go around popping cops."

"Smooth, are you okay? Aren't you forgetting that they are enemies too? Especially when it comes to them getting in the way of us getting money, bro," Sue reminded Smooth of their meeting instructions, which were preached by him.

"You're right. I'm tripping. I just want y'all niggas to be safe. That's all, bro. Do they have anybody?"

"Hell, naw, bro. We have the best on our team. We all family, nigga. Ain't nobody slipping. Feel me?" Sue Rabbit said.

"Is Guru good?"

"Yeah, Guru somewhere like me and where you need to be at with China. Booed up and cuddled up with your baby," Sue suggested.

"Man! She's tripping!"

"Why is that, bro?" Sue Rabbit asked.

"I went out looking for a nice house. It was $2.3 million, and she just blew up on me, after being happy and saying that it would alert the feds. But like I said, fuck the police!" Smooth explained to Sue while driving through traffic.

"I think you still need to be home, Smooth. Try to make it up to her. And as far as what she was saying about the feds coming snooping, she has a point. But if you want the castle for your queen, don't let her doubt stop you from making her sidewalk gold," Sue said.

"I feel that, bro. Thanks a lot!" Smooth replied.

"Family!" Sue Rabbit said as he hung up.

Smooth then called Amanda's phone.

"Hello."

"How many you've got left?"

"Just four of them."

"Okay, don't worry about them. We'll finish them tomorrow, baby."

"Okay so when will you come get me to take me home?"

"I'm on my way now. First, I want to take you out to eat, and then go kick back and watch us a movie," Smooth suggested.

"Are you serious, Smooth?" Amanda asked.

"Serious as a heartbeat!" Smooth said before hanging up.

I'll chill with number two tonight, and then come in to go to sleep. I really don't have time for China's arguing tonight, Smooth thought, realizing that China hadn't called him since she called about Jane's plumbing problem hours ago.

15

*C*hina looked at the clock glowing red on the nightstand and saw that it was 3:00 a.m. Tracy was in bed asleep next to her.

Where the fuck is Smooth? China thought as she slowly got out of bed and then walked into the living room. Zorro stirred from his sleep and began to follow her from the living room to the kitchen. She was hoping to find Smooth asleep on the sofa, but she didn't.

What the fuck is wrong with him? she thought, fed up as she poured herself a glass of 100 percent orange juice. Zorro began to growl and run toward the door.

"Calm down, Zorro. Don't be barking!" China said as the front door could be heard being unlocked.

When Zorro saw that it was Smooth, he jumped all over him, happy to see his master.

"Hey, boy! What's good?" Smooth exclaimed, pulling the dog by his jaws as Zorro stood on his back legs.

"It's three o'clock in the morning, Smooth. Why are you staying out? And please don't give me that trapping bullshit. Because ain't nobody out working when the feds are out looking for the killers," China whispered before starting to shout as she got up in his face.

Zorro sensed the negative energy and ran inside the kitchen. China was trying her best not to wake up Tracy.

"Listen, baby."

"Nigga, don't baby me! Smooth, you think a bitch about to be up losing sleep because you don't want to open your damn eyes?"

"China, please. Let's not go through this, okay?" Smooth begged.

"What the fuck you mean please don't go through this?" China exploded, pushing Smooth and almost knocking him over the turned-up rug.

"You watch it!" Smooth exploded.

"Or what, Smooth, huh? You want to beat my ass? Go ahead, nigga, because I am not stepping down. Prison and death are the only things out at three in the morning—and your muthafuckin' sideline bitches! Who the fuck do you take me for, huh?"

Before China could finish, Smooth grabbed her face with a death grip and looked her in her eyes, which were watery from crying.

He smells like a woman, she thought.

"I think you're a completely different person that I take for as my woman and best friend, China. Stop fighting with me 'bout craziness. You blow up about the smallest things," Smooth said as she pulled away and pushed him again.

"Get the fuck off me, nigga. I don't even use Rogue, and it's all over you, Smooth. I'm glad to know that you take me as a damn fool. What, your cooking girl showered herself in Rogue? Man, get out of my face!" China exclaimed as she stormed into the bedroom, waking up Tracy from her sleep.

She then began to grab clothes off the hangers in her closet.

"Tracy, let's go! I'm done. This nigga has the nerve to walk in here smelling like a damn bitch!" China screamed.

"Really, Smooth?" Tracy yelled.

"Stay the fuck out of this, Tracy! Please! She tripping!"

"Oh, now I'm tripping, nigga!" China erupted with a flood of tears streaming down her face.

"China, you're blowing up about nothing. Where the hell do you think you're going?"

"My place!"

Smack!

Before Tracy could get her words out, Smooth backhanded the taste out of her mouth, causing her to fly back onto the bed. The slap had her seeing stars, and the room was dead silent. Smooth looked at China, who could only stare at him in disbelief. She had never seen Smooth act violently toward any woman. When she looked over at Tracy, who was quiet and balled into the fetal position, she ran to her aid.

"Tracy, baby, are you okay?" China asked as she turned Tracy around and embraced her.

"I'm out! He hit me! I want out, China!" Tracy cried.

"We're both out!" China said coldly.

"Oh yeah?" Smooth said, staring at China with an evil look on his face.

China didn't know the man staring back at her, from Adam. Nor did he recognize the woman who had just decided to walk out of his life. They got through whatever together, and the only thing he could now transparently see was that Tracy had changed them completely from the very beginning. China would never admit it, but she had told Smooth how shit went down between them from day one, when he was in the hospital. Smooth saw that China loved Tracy more than the bond they had built from childhood. And that hurt him to his soul. There was no guilt trip to reproach with, nothing but a hole in his heart.

"I'm done, Smooth! I gave you plenty of heads up, yet you refused to pay attention. I used to dream of us being a happy family when I came home, yet I came home to you almost lying on your damn death bed. I asked you to leave the game alone. We have money to just be comfortable, but you want to be out there on the front lines with your niggas and do what the fuck you want to do, Smooth. I thought we would get married, and you haven't asked me yet. Smooth, I'm in love with Tracy, and that's all I'm focused on. I am done with men!" China said, looking Smooth in his eyes.

Smooth walked up to China and stared her in the eyes.

"You're leaving me for a woman, huh?" Smooth asked her.

"Yeah, I'm leaving you for a woman! Now put your hands on me, Smooth. I swear you'll regret it!"

"Just like you will regret losing a real nigga, China! When I return, I don't want to see you or your bitch in here."

"You won't. I promise you that!" China replied.

Before he exploded further on China, Smooth turned on his heels and left the apartment. He was furious and couldn't believe his ears. China had left him for a lot of reasons. He had no one for a mentor but one person. Smooth walked down to Miranda's apartment and knocked on her door. He waited patiently for the door to open. When it did, Miranda stood there looking sexy as hell in her pajamas, with her arms crossed over her chest.

"What's the problem? It's almost four o'clock in the morning," Miranda whispered.

"You were right, Miranda."

"What are you talking about, Smooth?" Miranda asked in a whisper.

"She left me and declared her love for Tracy!" Smooth sighed and then badly wanted to get out of the hallway. "Can I come in?"

"Not tonight, Smooth. I have company," Miranda said, being honest with him.

That's why she's whispering, huh, Smooth thought.

"Damn! When did this happen?"

Really? Miranda thought.

"Smooth, listen. We're friends. I have no obligation to tell you who it is I'm sharing my bed with. I'm not the one to stick around and wait on a dream to come true. Come back when the sun comes up, and we will talk," Miranda told him.

"I feel that! Sorry for waking you, Miranda."

"It's okay, Smooth. You did nothing wrong. Just come back in the morning, and we can talk, okay?"

"Yeah," Smooth replied as he walked away from the door a sad puppy.

He didn't want to head back to his place and be alone, so he got inside his Range Rover, pulled out his phone, and called up his newest frustration pad.

"Hello."

"What are you doing, beautiful?" Smooth asked.

"I'm just sitting up thinking about you, handsome."

"Oh really?"

"Something like that!"

"I'm coming over so we can both think together," Smooth said.

"Okay," Jane replied, eager to get back in the sack with Smooth.

* * *

Tracy couldn't believe that Smooth had put his hands on her. Little did he know that she was used to black eyes and busted lips. Putting his hands on her was a grave mistake. She now had his bitch, and she wouldn't let China run back to him if she had to kill her herself. Together, she and China packed up all that they could and went over to Tracy's apartment in North Miami. Tracy might have taken a hit from Smooth, but she had won, and he had taken a loss. Any baller in Miami would drop their entire squad of females to be with China.

And here it was, the dumbass taking shit as a game! Tracy thought as she lay in bed with China in her arms.

China was still up and could sense that Tracy was as well. Tracy was one of a whirlwind of thoughts in China's mind.

"What are you thinking about?" China asked.

"I'm just thinking how dumb he is letting you get away."

"He didn't let me get away, remember? We walked away together."

"Are you serious about letting him go, China?"

"I don't know. My soul says yes, but my heart is indecisive. He's all I know."

"And he's hurt you by not considering your heart, baby," Tracy said to China as she sat up in bed and crossed her arms.

China looked up at Tracy and saw her split busted lip.

"I can't believe he hit you."

"There's a first time for everything. If it wasn't me, then he would have hit you!" Tracy said.

China wasn't a gullible person. There wasn't anything that Tracy could possibly say to make her believe that Smooth would have put his hands on her. China knew why Smooth had slapped Tracy.

He doesn't love her like he loves me, China thought.

"I don't think he would have put his hands on me, baby. But I could never say never or not put it past any man. It's just we've been together too long," China said.

"And now you have new love and new meaning. You don't have to worry about me coming home. Not everyone who has a childhood sweetheart lives with their childhood sweetheart forever, baby. If it was forever, then we wouldn't love each other today. Since day one, you've been hurting and worried about one day becoming a damn widow because he don't know how to be a real boss like Juan and let his friends and workers handle business. If he would have bought that big-ass house for $2.3 million, what convincing did he do to prove that we wouldn't be left in the big-ass house alone?" Tracy asked.

She has a point, China thought as she laid her head in Tracy's lap.

Tracy immediately began to run her fingers through China's locks.

"I just don't want to be hurt, China. If you're done, then be done! If not, then at least let me know. Woman, I love you so much. You're the best thing that has ever happened to me," Tracy said as the inevitable tears fell from her eyes and onto China's face.

China sat up and gently kissed Tracy on her busted lip. Tracy had nothing on but a T-shirt. China slowly removed it and began sucking on her erect brown nipples.

"Mmmmm!" Tracy moaned out as China sucked on both nipples slowly and passionately.

China came back up and kissed Tracy's teary face. She licked her tears like a dog licks his wounds.

"Don't cry," China begged into Tracy's ear as she began sucking on her ears and neck.

"Okay, baby!" Tracy purred. "I love you, China."

"I love you too, beautiful," China said as she descended Tracy's body, planting kisses until she came to the wet mount between Tracy's legs.

China spread apart her pussy lips and began sucking and licking on her walls.

"Mmmm!" Tracy purred when China stuck two fingers inside her and then began finger fucking her and sucking on her clit. "Yes, baby!"

"Who's pussy is this?"

"Yours, baby! Yours!"

"Who is yours, bitch?"

"China, baby! This is your pussy!" Tracy moaned out as China rapidly fist fucked her. "Oh my gosh! That shit feels so good, China. Mmmmm!"

"You love me, baby?" China asked.

"Yes, I do, baby. I love you so much!"

"I love you too, baby, okay?"

"Yes, baby. I'm coming!" Tracy panted loudly.

"I know you are. Now come all over this fist, baby!" China ordered.

"Oh shit, baby! I'm coming!" Tracy shrilled in ecstasy as she came to her orgasm.

When China saw that Tracy was convulsing, she pulled her fist out of Tracy's pussy and let her lick her hand clean.

"Mmmmm!" China moaned as she and Tracy licked her hand like an ice cream cone. "I love you, baby," China said.

"I love you too, baby," Tracy replied.

16

*I*t seemed that the sun came up at the same moment that Smooth had collapsed and closed his eyes after fucking Jane for an hour straight, from foreplay to deep penetration. Jane woke up Smooth to get on his way. She got what she wanted; now it was time for her to be on her way to work.

"Smooth, boy, get yo ass up before you get caught up," Jane warned Smooth, who threw the pillow over his head, too tired to move out of bed.

Jane had no car and was restricted from driving for five years after her release from prison. So she caught a ride to work with Tabby every morning.

I bet he get his ass up when he hear his bitch name, Jane thought.

"China is on her way to bring me to work, boy."

"Say what?" Smooth shouted as he sprung from the bed and started putting on his clothes in a hurry.

"Do it look like I'd be standing here if it was her. My girl Tabby is coming, and I don't need her to be all in my business," Jane explained.

"Alright. Um, just call me later when you get off."

"So you'll be back tonight?" she asked.

"Of course I will. We locked in, ma," Smooth said as he leaned down and kissed her on her sexy lips.

"Okay," Jane said as she melted in the aftermath of his kiss.

Damn, I'm feeling this nigga. If only he knew there's no way out, Jane thought as she watched Smooth put on his bulletproof vest and leave.

When he was gone, Jane hurried to the bathroom and opened her medicine cabinet. She grabbed her pill bottle and then popped her daily medications for her illness. After washing the pills down, she walked into her kitchen and poured herself a glass of milk. She loved milk because besides her medication, dairy was one of the products that kept her weight up. When she heard Tabby's horn, she hurried out of the apartment feeling like a million bucks.

"Girl, why you so damn happy this morning? You must've got you some dick!" Tabby said to a gleeful Jane.

"The man of my dreams paid a visit to me, that's all!"

"And who is that?" Tabby asked.

"If I tell you, then I'll have to kill you. And I don't want to kill a good friend of mine."

"Well, keep it to yourself. Guess what? I have some good news!"

"What? You lost weight or gained more ass?" Jane joked.

"No, silly, it's nothing like that. Well, it could serve as an element to gaining weight, I guess," Tabby responded.

"Well, what is it? I'm burnt out and don't have the energy to be guessing, homegirl."

"I'm pregnant!" Tabby spit out.

"Get the fuck out of here, girl! That is wonderful news. Who's the daddy?"

"If I tell you, I'll have to kill you." Tabby laughed.

"Whatever, bitch!" Jane replied, with a smile on her face.

"Girl, you already know I ain't fucking nobody but Money's insecure ass. That nigga will kill me if I fuck another nigga," Tabby announced as she turned into the restaurant parking lot.

At 7:00 a.m., Roxy and Nicole had the place running, and it was already booming with business.

"Pretty soon, Roxy gonna have to open up another restaurant. Shit! Her business be drawing people all the way from South Beach!" Jane explained.

"Yeah, then we could be managers at the other one."

"Roxy too smart not to be already thinking like that," Tabby added.

"I'ma see. Shit! I'd think she would make China run one of them before anybody else, right?" Jane asked.

"I would if it was my sister and plans," Tabby said as she parked then stepped out of the car.

Together, Jane and Tabby walked through the door and clocked in.

"Good morning you two chicken heads!" Roxy said to the women.

"She's pregnant."

"Jane!" Tabby exclaimed, not appreciating Jane putting her business out there so early.

"Well, I'll be damned! Is it true?"

"Yes, it's true, Roxy. I should be the one announcing it," Tabby said.

"Girl, you know a bitch can't hold water!" Roxy said.

"Yeah, I guess. Where's China and Tracy?" Tabby asked, not seeing either of them on the clock.

"They're on their way now," Roxy said as she walked off to take a customer's order. "Let's get to work, ladies."

* * *

Smooth arrived at his apartment tired and exhausted. On his way up on the elevator, all he could think about was China.

How the fuck did I lose my girl for years to a bitch she just met? I guess it's true that love is like a bullet. It has no name on it, meaning anybody could get it, Smooth thought.

He knew that half of the problem was him fucking up, but he couldn't help it. If he hadn't put his hands on Tracy, it would have been the same result.

Shit! China was packing her things before I hit Tracy in her shit! Smooth thought as the elevator doors opened.

When Smooth stepped off the elevator, he saw two Mexican men cleaning the big window down toward where his apartment was located. He could hear Zorro barking as he got closer. Nothing struck him as amiss, being that his mind was so trained on China.

It's time for me to take Zorro for a walk, Smooth thought as he neared his door.

When Smooth made it to the door, just as he was about to insert the key, something prompted him to take a double take at the men. He could now hear Zorro growling. Using his peripheral vision, Smooth saw one of the Mexicans making a move. He only had a split second to react, and timed the movement exactly. Smooth stuck the key into the door, pushed it open with one hand, and reached for his Glock .40. As the door opened, he fell to the floor but was able to squeeze off two quick shots, hitting the Mexican who was creeping up on him.

The second Mexican pulled out a TEC-9 from the bucket and sprayed Smooth's apartment. Smooth was back on his feet by this time. As he was running with Zorro behind, bullets bounced off the living room walls. The Mexican assassin came further into the apartment in search of Smooth. When he walked into the kitchen, he shot blindly until he saw that it was empty. Smooth couldn't believe it.

These muthafuckin' Mexicans are getting bolder each day that passes, he thought as he hid from the man in his bedroom closet.

He had a good angle and view of the bedroom door if the killer did come looking for him there.

Come on, man. It's too early to be playing these games! Smooth thought as he waited for the Mexican to walk through the bedroom door.

"Smooth, mi amigo!" the assassin called out in a deep voice.

At least he knows that he's at the right address, Smooth thought as he trained the gun toward the entrance of the door while Zorro hid under the bed growling at the assassin.

Don't blow our cover, Zorro! Smooth thought.

"Smooth, mi amigo!" the assassin called again.

Smooth could hear the hall bathroom door being kicked open. He was close.

"Come on, stupid Mexican," Smooth whispered to himself, anticipating the Mexican's appearance in his bedroom.

Smooth was sweating excessively as he awaited the Mexican coming through the door.

"Smooth, mi—"

Boom! Boom! Boom! Boom!

The shots were distinctive from the TEC-9, and Smooth easily picked up on it. As soon as he was about to make his move, Smooth heard the call of victory.

"Smooth!" China called out for him.

"I'm in here with Zorro!"

When China rushed into the room with a smoking Glock .40, she stood in the doorway with an evil look on her face.

"Do you still think $2.3 million is too much to move?"

"Smooth, you can move anywhere you want. Like I told you, I'm done with you. I'm just here to get my work clothes. You better be glad I keep this baby with me," she said while holding up her Glock.

"Isn't that the twin to mine?'

"Yeah, and you're not getting it back!"

"China, do you gotta do this? You're tripping for real."

"Smooth, it's too late to try to talk about anything. You're staying out late, coming in smelling like another bitch, and got too much love for your damned homeboys. I'm done, and I mean with men—period! At least I'm not leaving you for another man!" China said as she grabbed her work clothes and then strutted out of the room and apartment.

Damn! I think I fucked up! Smooth thought regretfully.

Smooth picked up his iPhone from the closet floor and called his cleanup crew.

"Yo!"

"I need the cleanup crew sent to my apartment," Smooth said to Big Mitch.

"I got ya, bro."

"Alright!" Smooth answered as he hung up the phone.

"Zorro, we have to move. It's no longer safe here, boy," Smooth said to his dog, who climbed on top of the bed and lay down next to Smooth, who was sitting on the edge of the bed.

The $2.3 million is definitely about to go toward the house, with or without China, Smooth thought.

When his phone rang, Smooth answered on the first ring. "Hello."

"Good news or the real good news?" Spencer's voice boomed through the phone.

"Either one is better than being almost killed by an assassin," Smooth replied.

"When was this?"

"Shit! Just a few minutes ago!"

"Where?" Spencer asked.

"At my damn apartment!"

"Damn! But, yeah, the good news is I got a Mexican that knows how to speak English, and this muthafucka is definitely talking English," Spencer told him.

"That's damn good news, bro! I'm ready to take it to these muthafuckas hard," Smooth announced.

"Just know that you are not alone, bro. I'm here for you."

"Thanks. I really appreciate that."

"I promised the two Mexicans that I won't kill them if they talk. But I also told them that I would do what my boss says. So if you want them out, let me know, and I'll get rid of them," Spencer said.

"Where are you?"

"I'm at the pad."

"Keep them there. Once I get this mess cleaned up, I'll be over there," Smooth told him, and then hung up.

Smooth was fortunate that everyone in his vicinity was at their jobs. No one ever heard the war zone in his apartment. There were no sirens and no witnesses.

"I could have been a baked chicken if not for China," Smooth said to himself as the cleanup crew arrived.

"I don't want to ever see them again. Take 'em to the Everglades," Smooth ordered.

"Yes sir, boss."

"Come on, Zorro!" Smooth called out as he clipped on the leash and they walked out the door.

* * *

"Damn, Jane. You okay? It's not like you to be so damn quiet," China asked.

"Nah, girl. I'm just thinking of some shit in my past."

"Damn, he was that bad!" China said, getting a laugh going.

"You're crazy, China! I'm good, though. What about you? Your ass came in here all mad and shit!" Jane acknowledged.

"Yeah, I was. But I'm good now. It's no pressure. I just stopped fucking with Smooth."

"Girl, get the fuck out of here! What happen?" Jane exclaimed.

"It's a long story."

And my gain now! Jane thought, instantly realizing how much time she and Smooth could spend booed up. *Shit! He minds anyway. It's too late to pull out now!*

China went on to explain her and Smooth's breakup and her new beginning. There was no way that Smooth could take back the mistake, even if he tried to.

Eventually, I would have gotten him. And now with this good news, I just know it's all for a reason that I met Smooth, she reflected.

* * *

Smooth pulled up to the slaughter pad and parked behind Spencer's silver Camaro Z28. Next to it sat Spencer's old Dodge van. Smooth stepped out of his Range Rover with Zorro and then walked into the abandoned building. All the windows were boarded up, and all the exits and entries were secured. When Smooth got to the main door, Spencer had to unfasten the chain on the door.

"So you brought Zorro, huh?" Spencer asked while rubbing Zorro on his head.

"Yeah, I couldn't leave him in the mess. So I brought him along," Smooth said while looking at the two teens hanging from a joist and bound by their hands, two feet off the ground.

"Are both of them talking?" Smooth inquired as Tic came through a side door with a chainsaw in his hands.

"Yeah, both of them are talking."

"Come, Zorro!" Smooth called as he unleashed his dog, who immediately ran over to sniff the boys.

"He can smell the fear on 'em," Smooth said as he walked toward the teens.

"It's cutting through the air like a knife on butter," Spencer said.

"Tic, we meet again," Smooth said as he shook Tic's hand.

"How are you, boss?"

"I'm ready to get this show running. What 'bout you?" Smooth asked.

Tic then riled up the chainsaw with an evil smirk on his face. Zorro began to growl at the sound.

"Zorro, calm down!" Smooth called as his dog immediately lay down on the ground.

Smooth then walked closer to the teens and looked the first one in his eyes.

"What's your name, Mexican?"

"Julio."

"How old are you?"

"I'm seventeen."

"So you know where to find Juan?"

"I know his father. He owns a Mexican joint on 33rd. Juan comes every Friday to pick up his money and drop off more cocaine for his dad," Julio explained.

Smooth then walked to the second boy and looked him in the eyes.

"What's your name?"

"Dias."

"How old are you, Dias?"

"I'm seventeen. I'm turning eighteen next week."

"Do you know where to find Juan?"

"Yes, just like Julio told you. He comes by every Friday to get his money."

"Are you two M-13s?"

"Yes, we are M-13s."

Smooth looked at Tic and then gave him the green light. "Tic! Legs, arms, head. Dispose of them!" Smooth ordered, and then walked away. "Come, Zorro!" Smooth called out as the chainsaw riled up.

"Nooooo! Please! Arggghhh!" Julio screamed as Tic sawed off his left leg.

The boy was killed instantly when Tic then took the saw and ran it down the center of his torso.

17

*C*hoppa and Mall were back on 112th as soon as the crime scene cleared up, just like they planned. There was no more unmarkeds sitting on the block. Money was coming left and right, and the trap house was like an ice cream truck stopping in the hood.

"Yo, I'm hungry as hell! I'ma go to the Jamaican restaurant on 12th. You want something?" Choppa asked Mall, who was sitting on the sofa in the trap watching the Dolphins get their asses beat by Tampa Bay.

"Yeah, go ahead and get me that jerk chicken special," Mall said as he pulled a wad out of his jeans and gave Choppa a twenty-dollar bill.

"When Money gets back, tell that nigga to go pick up our ARs from Phat Zoe in Lil Haiti," Choppa reminded Mall.

"Okay. I'ma go ahead and do that, bro," Mall said as he then looked at his time on his Rolex. "It's eight o'clock now. Try to be back before nine!"

"I'ma be back before that," Choppa said as he walked out the front door.

* * *

"Yellow!"

"Cuzo, I need some help over here," Ham said.

"Talk to me. What's good?"

"Trap is booming. I need like fourteen ounces."

"Give me an hour, cuzo, and I'll be 'round there," Banga promised.

"Okay. I'll be here," Ham said as he then hung up the phone.

Tina was at a doctor's appointment and wouldn't be back until nine o'clock, being that she was driving from Miami. She was with her cousin Janye, who Ham trusted and with whom he approved for her to associate. Ham sat at the kitchen table in his and Tina's one-bedroom apartment and finished up counting his re-up money. When he was done, he took the crumbs of his crack from inside his pill bottle and laced his weed inside a Philly blunt. After rolling the crack-weed blunt, Ham took his lighter and put flame to the blunt. Ham inhaled the smoke, choked on it a bit, and then took another hit.

"That's right! Good shit!" Ham said as he put the blunt out on the table.

Ham was high as a muthafucka! He couldn't help smoking his product. Ever since he started for the first time two months ago, he became hooked. He had no clue that Tina was using again, and neither did she nor anyone else know that he was now using his own product. To kill the smell before Banga made it over to drop off his product, Ham sprayed cologne and then began frying eggs to satisfy his munchies. Before Ham could finish cooking, he grabbed the blunt again, lit it from the heat on the stove, hit it twice, and then put it out again. He was definitely hooked.

* * *

Inside the Jamaican restaurant on 12th, Choppa had his eyes on a bad-ass big booty Jamaican waitress who couldn't keep her eyes off him either. When the waitress walked past him to go clean out her bucket and refill it with new water, Choppa made his move and stepped in front of her.

"Two eyes always watching each other establish our first thing in common," Choppa said in his smoothest mac game.

"Oh yeah? Why you tink I'm watching you, mon?"

"By that smile you're trying to hide on your face," Choppa replied.

"Whatever, mon!"

"What's your name?" Choppa asked.

"Bree."

"Choppa, Bree," he introduced as he offered his hand with his number folded on a small piece of paper.

"You plan good, huh?" Bree asked.

"Naw, I'm just always ahead of the game, ma," Choppa replied.

"I hear you. I'll give you a call, Choppa. Right now I have to get back to work. See you later," Bree said while blushing as she turned around and walked away.

"Yeah, I'll see that phat-ass booty later too," Choppa said as he stepped up in line to order his food.

After ordering, Choppa blew a kiss to Bree, who smiled. He then walked outside to his baby-blue Chevy Impala on twenty-eight-inch custom rims. Choppa then turned up the thunderous bass to the Rick Ross/Meek Mills hit and pulled off into traffic. He was feeling good about himself, especially since fucking with Smooth had gotten him on a high level of getting money. Mall was the key that got him and Money through the door.

Before Choppa and Money started slanging dope, they were Miami's finest jack boys. They didn't care who they robbed; when the gun came out and a nigga didn't hit the ground, his brains were left on the pavement for CSI.

When Choppa came to a red light, he dug inside his bag of food for a piece of chicken. He never saw the van pull up alongside him, or three ski-masked Mexicans who had hopped out with M-16s. One of them opened Choppa's door, and it was too late for him to react.

"What the?"

Bam!

Before Choppa could say anything else, he was struck in the temple with the butt of an M-16 rifle and knocked completely out. The Mexicans braked the car and slammed it into park before the car could roll. Before the light turned green, Choppa was abducted and knocked out cold in the back of the van.

* * *

China and Tracy were getting off work and walking to China's Mercedes, when Smooth pulled up and parked directly behind her, blocking in her car. Both China and Tracy rolled their eyes, not wanting to be bothered by him.

"China, can I talk to you? Both of you?"

"I have nothing to say to you, Smooth," Tracy said as she got in the car.

"What do you want, Smooth?"

"It's not dawning on me. All I ask is that you hear me out."

"China, hear me out. Is that what you're telling me?"

"Yes, I am!"

"But damn, Smooth, what happened when you wouldn't hear me out, huh? When I told you how to handle your damn empire? You can't love the streets and your queen, Smooth. I meant what I said, Smooth," China said.

"You're being blinded. This is not you. From day one, I noticed."

"From day one, I lost a childhood sweetheart. It was only a matter of time to see that I was tripping. Smooth, you could have lost your damn life! Instead of coming home with a different game plan, you came home with the same one that landed you in the hospital. I don't want no part of it," China said while looking Smooth in his eyes.

"I'm sorry, China," he said as he walked up to her, reached into his pocket, and came out with a velvet box.

He opened the lid and showed China a big-ass diamond rock.

"One more chance. I promise I won't fuck up, China."

China looked at the rock with tears cascading down her face. When she looked in the car at Tracy, she saw Tracy shaking her head left and right. China looked at the ring while swiping tears away, and then back at Smooth. He could tell that she still loved him unconditionally. It was the ring she had been looking for, and yet she was shaking her head no.

"I can't, Smooth. It's over," China said as she got into her Mercedes, leaving Smooth standing alone.

Smooth looked toward the restaurant and saw Roxy from inside, looking at him. She threw her hands up in pity for him. She knew China well. When her mind was made, it was made!

Damn, I fucked up! Smooth thought as he jumped back into his truck and pulled off.

* * *

When China and Tracy made it home, they made love and then fell asleep to a movie. They were exhausted and drowning in each other's love. Tracy emerged from bed and left China still asleep. She grabbed her phone and then walked into the living room. Tracy sat cross-legged on the sofa and called Juan, who picked up on the second ring.

"Hola!"

"Why is he still walking, Juan?"

"Woman, I can't help that the Negro is smart."

"Juan, please get him out of my life," Tracy said.

"I will, bonita. Don't worry. We got this, okay? You find out where he's laying his head at," Juan instructed her.

"Okay, I will do that."

"*Te amo*, bonita," Juan replied.

"Yeah, whatever!" Tracy said before she disconnected the call.

Kill him and kill him fast! Tracy thought.

* * *

After seeing the abduction of Choppa on the news, Mall became furious. No one could identify the abductors as the Mexicans, but Mall—and everyone else—knew that their enemies were responsible. At the trap house, Smooth called an emergency meeting of all his high-ranking soldiers.

"These crackas ain't gonna do no justice nor look for Choppa. So we gonna play the game how it's supposed to be played. Choppa is family, and we going to show these Mexicans that he is indeed our family," Smooth said to everyone gathered in the living room.

He looked around at everyone's faces and saw the grief all over Mall.

"Remember, for every one of us they take, we take three of them down!" Smooth reminded all of them by holding up three fingers.

"Dat's right," one of the Smooth's lieutenants, Jay, said.

"Let's go get these muthafuckas, my nigga!" Smooth said as he racked his AK-47.

"Hell yeah, my nigga!" Big Mitch shouted and then racked his.

Everyone in the room racked their AK-47s, ready to go out and shed blood for Choppa. Mall just couldn't figure out how Choppa had let the Mexicans creep up on him.

What the fuck was he doing? Mall thought as everyone in the room filed out of the trap house to go make the streets bleed.

* * *

"Mmmm! Shit. Fuck me, daddy!" Jane shouted out as her sugar daddy named Marvin fucked her hard from the back.

Marvin was a known trick from North Miami, who everyone knew had full-blown AIDS. For months, he had been fucking Jane on her demand, and then he'd leave her with a large sum of money. She loved giving herself to Marvin. He was able to hit all the spots that no other man could hit since she had been home from prison. In fact, she had fucked over thirty different men thus far.

"I'm coming, daddy!" Jane screamed while looking back at Marvin with a facial expression that caused Marvin to explode inside of her phat, excessively wet pussy.

"Uhhh shit!" he yelled.

"That's right, daddy. This yo puss. Skeet all in me, big-dick muthafucka!" Jane exclaimed.

When Marvin collapsed on the bed, Jane grabbed his dick and sucked him clean before she lay down next to him.

"Why do you fuck me so good?"

"Because yo pussy is too good."

"Are you coming back next week?" Jane asked.

"Baby, I'm coming whenever you call me. Don't I always come?"

"Yeah, you do, daddy. Your birthday is next week too. I swear you don't look forty-five years old," she told him.

"I don't feel it either," Marvin replied.

"Well, that means I still got some work to do," Jane said as she climbed on top of him and rode his cock.

* * *

When Smooth, Sue Rabbit, and Guru stepped into the Mexican joint on 33rd, the small hole-in-the-wall bar was crowded. Mexican music emanated from an old jukebox, and everyone was intoxicated at some level. As the threesome sat down at the bar, a beautiful bartender walked over to them.

"May I help you?" she said to Smooth in good English.

"Yeah, let me get a shot of Mexican rum, bonita," Smooth shouted over the loud music while leaning into the bar so she could hear him. "We all want the same. All drinks on me," Smooth announced.

"Okay, handsome," the bartender said as she walked off to fix drinks for the threesome.

When she got to the shelf, she saw the red light flashing on the telephone. Smooth, Sue Rabbit, and Guru all saw it too.

"He sees us!" Smooth said to Sue, whose hands were already gripping his MAC-10, ready to turn the small-capacity Mexican joint into mayhem.

Smooth was the only one who saw the bartender looking at him and his two homeboys through the glass in front of her. When she hung up the phone, Smooth looked at his watch, and then all hell broke loose. Mall, Money, and Big

Mitch burst through the doors with ski masks and AK-47s and took down everything and everyone in their paths.

Chop! Chop! Chop! Chop!

Sue Rabbit and Guru raised up with their MAC-10s and joined the rest. Smooth kept his eye on the bartender, who ducked behind the counter screaming for her life.

Smooth jumped over the counter and pulled out his Glock .22. He rushed over to the bartender, who was trembling and afraid, and snatched her up by her hair, placing the gun to her head. The place was wild and sounded like a cross-seas battlefield.

"Please don't kill me!"

"Where the fuck is Juan Sr.?"

"He's in the back," the bartender said, just as Smooth looked up and saw Sue Rabbit and Guru making their way to the back.

"Where's Juan Jr.?"

"I don't know. I promise. I don't know. He only comes on Fridays lately. He hasn't been coming."

When Smooth looked up again, he saw Sue Rabbit and Guru bringing an old man from the back, jacked up by the back of his suit coat.

"Is that Juan Sr.?" Smooth asked the bartender, turning her head toward the old man.

"Yes, that's him!" she said.

"Where are the tapes?"

"In his office under his desk."

"Come on," Smooth said as he dragged her to Juan Sr.'s office and made her retrieve the tapes to the hidden cameras.

"Please don't kill me. I'll be your wife, and I don't know."

Boom! Boom! Boom!

"I know you don't know nothing," Smooth said after shooting the bartender three times in the head, sending her brains flying everywhere on Juan Sr.'s oak desk.

18

Juan couldn't believe his ears that his father's joint was ambushed and that his father was abducted. He knew deep down that it was only the art of war and retaliation. Juan knew that abducting Choppa would bring such aftermath. But he never would have thought that his father would be the product of his now realized mistake.

He walked into the room where Choppa was bound to a chair and covered in blood from being beaten with a spiked chain. He was completely disfigured. Mario was having a lot of fun beating him up, until Juan delivered him the news over the phone. Juan had ordered Mario to cease the torture. Walking up to Choppa, Juan could only imagine what would be done to his father if Smooth saw how Choppa looked.

Damn, man, this Negro is almost dead! Juan thought.

An AMBER Alert was still out for Choppa throughout Miami and the surrounding area. Juan and Mario had Choppa at an abandoned junkyard inside one of the offices. It was the last place the police would come searching for an abducted drug dealer like they had broadcast on the news the moment they discovered his identity.

"You are a famous man, Choppa!" Juan said to him. Choppa's eyes were swollen shut and he could only hear in one ear.

"Are you ready to go home?" Juan asked Choppa, who nodded his head up and down, unable to speak from the broken jaw that Mario had given him.

"Are you still going to protect Smooth?"

Choppa again shook his head up and down. He wasn't breaking. It didn't matter how much he'd been beaten up and subsequently knocked unconscious. He wasn't giving up Smooth.

"This man has a big heart, esé," Mario said.

"Yeah, a stupid one too!" Juan replied.

"So, what's the deal?" Mario asked.

"We wait until they call us," Juan instructed.

* * *

"Come on, old man! You saying you don't speak no English, huh?" Smooth said to Juan Sr., who was hanging from the joist and bound at his wrists.

Now he was a frightened sixty-five-year-old man, but he was a legendary gangsta in his prime.

"No English!" Juan Sr. said again.

"Spencer, I think you could make this muthafucka speak some English!" Smooth said while puffing on a Cuban cigar.

"I hate them kinds," Spencer said, sitting on a metal table swinging his legs. "I think we could give him a couple tattoos," he suggested.

"So you don't know the code to your phone, huh?" Smooth asked the old man, who was now sweating intensely.

I hope I don't give the man a heart attack before we get what we need out of him, Smooth thought.

"No English!" he screamed.

Smooth was getting frustrated. No English seemed like the only word Juan Sr. knew, and Smooth knew better. He didn't want to give the man a heart attack, but something had to give or take. So Smooth took the burning cigar and placed it under Juan Sr.'s armpits.

"Arrgghhh! No English!" Juan Sr. screamed as Smooth put out his cigar under his arm.

"Number to code is what?" Smooth asked.

"2301," he responded in almost perfect English.

Everyone in the room exploded into laughter as Smooth entered the code to unlock the old man's phone.

"You're really about to pay for that. You want to lie and play games? We will do just that, papi!" Smooth said while looking for Juan Jr.'s phone number, but also facing a language barrier.

"Where is Juan's number, old man?"

"786-447-2013," he answered, directing Smooth through his phone.

Juan Sr. had caught on quickly. Smooth didn't want him; he wanted his only son, and Juan Sr. had just given him up. When Smooth found the digits, he smiled and was eager to hear Mr. Juan José's voice for the first time. Smooth dialed the number on a disposable phone and got Juan on the line immediately.

"Who is this?"

"Your muthafuckin' nightmare!" Smooth said.

"Uhhh, it's you, huh? Or is this one of your soldiers?"

"You knew who would be calling you, and you knew that it would be a piece of cake to get it out of your old man. It's funny how I was able to teach him English."

"Man, don't hurt my dad, boy. If you do, I swear I'll hit home base with you, Negro!" Juan exclaimed.

Smooth had missed the understatement. He was too excited to know that he had Juan where he needed him to be.

"So tell me. Why would you play the abducting game if you can't stand the heat?" Smooth asked Juan, who he imagined rubbing his temples in distress.

"Okay, man. You got the prize. So I have something of yours, and you have something of mine, homie. So let's do what we are supposed to do," Juan suggested.

"And where is my man, Choppa?"

"Choppa is okay, my friend. Let's just say you've come on time. No harm to my father, and no harm to your friend."

"Keep it like that. You let Choppa go, and then we'll definitely let your father go." Smooth sounded convincing.

Juan thought for a moment to get a good game plan going.

Choppa is just about dead already. He is losing too much blood. So things have to be calculated to work out smoothly, Juan thought.

"Do you know where the gym is on 37th? Send your men with my father, and I'll send my men."

"No, Juan. I want you, chico!" Smooth exploded.

"It'll never happen, Smooth. Two things about me that you lack: a chance and vulnerability. That is what makes us two different people, my friend."

"I'ma tell you like this, Juan. You play games, and I will make sure your father is the next example!" Smooth threatened.

"I will deal you a fair hand, just as long as your cards are all showing on the table. Meet my men at the old gym on 37th, with my father, at twelve o'clock sharp. It's eleven now, so we both have an hour," Juan explained as he disconnected the call.

"The old gym on 37th, Sue Rabbit. Call Mall and get some men over there now!" Smooth ordered.

"I got you, bro."

"Spencer, stay on point," Smooth ordered his man, who was still sitting on the table swinging his legs.

"I got you, Smooth. Me and Tic are about to have some fun," Spencer said, with an evil smirk on his face while looking at Juan Sr., who appeared scared to death.

* * *

China was worried about Smooth, despite showing him differently.

People are being abducted, and Smooth is vulnerable, China thought.

All day she had been thinking about the ring he showed her but that she had declined to take.

Did I make a mistake? I can understand Tracy's reason for not wanting to be back in his life. But, damn, am I making a mistake by leaving the true love of my life for a new love? China contemplated as she lay in bed with Tracy asleep in her arms.

I can't hurt Tracy for someone who's hurt the both of us, she thought, settling her indecisiveness with that conclusion.

Tracy was too good to her. China now only had to find a way to bring her love for Jenny into the picture.

I will. China got this. Jenny, China, and Tracy, China thought as she closed her eyes with a smile on her face.

* * *

Mall and Money made it over to the gym with a couple of their soldiers, and found the building empty.

"No one's arrived yet," Money said while looking out into the night behind the broken windows. It was 11:45 p.m., and Juan's men were supposed to show within the next fifteen minutes.

"I still don't know how the fuck Choppa let the muthafuckas get him, man. He's too damn on beat to be slippin'!" Money said to Mall.

"We don't know what the fuck happened. Let's just pray that we can ask him, and that these chicos deliver bro safe."

"Yeah! Let's hope they do. If not, they think we doing something now, I'ma drop everyone that looks like a wetback!" Money expressed.

When Mall and everyone saw the headlights appear at the back of the gym lot, they immediately killed all the lights. Everyone got into position and ran toward a broken or shattered window.

"They driving a black van, bro," Jay said as he looked out.

Mall's phone vibrated in his pocket. He grabbed it and answered, "Yo!"

"Is everything clear?" Sue Rabbit asked.

"Yeah, we're looking at them now. They pulled up in a black van."

"Are they flickering their lights?"

Mall looked over, and the headlights were indeed turning off and on.

"Yeah, their lights are flashing."

"That's us. We're coming in," Sue Rabbit said, and then hung up the phone.

"That's our men," Mall told everyone, who were ready to squeeze the triggers at any crazy movement.

* * *

Juan had his men dress Choppa in all black so no one could see his bloody body. He was constantly fading in and out of consciousness from losing so much blood that was pouring from his wounds.

"Esé, I don't think he's gonna make it," Tito said to Javier, who was driving the SUV and trying to get to the location in a hurry.

Behind them were three other SUVs full of their M-13 brothers, all ready to war it out with Smooth's men.

"The next corner, bro. Slow down before you miss it," Tito told Javier.

At the corner, Javier turned into the gym parking lot and pulled around back. When he saw the black van, he slowed down and kept his headlights on.

"They're here, esé!" Javier said, putting the SUV in park.

Javier had Juan's phone in his hand. He was just about to call the number from which Smooth called, when suddenly his phone rang first.

"It's them!" Javier said as he looked into his rear-view mirror and saw his brothers lined up behind him waiting on the word.

"Answer, homie!" Tito said.

"What's up?" Javier answered.

"You know what's up, homie! Let our man go, and we'll let your man go," Smooth said.

"Where is he?"

"That's not what I said. Please tell me you understand English as well as you speak it."

"I understand good English, Negro!" Javier said.

"Name calling now?"

Boom!

"Call me another insult, and I'll put the next bullet between ya man's eyes. Do we understand each other?" Smooth shouted.

"Man, listen. We gonna bring him out to y'all. He's highly wasted, so he won't be able to walk until he sobers up. When we drop him half distance, we want our man to walk out of the building," Javier informed Smooth.

"Why did you bring all of your lil friends with you?" Smooth asked. "We are only three deep."

"Let's take 'em!" Tito whispered.

"We always ride deep. Something your boy should have done. Maybe he wouldn't be in the position he's in today."

"Mmmm!" Choppa moaned, trying to speak.

"See, your boy is trying to get sober now. We move first, and then you move. We'll lay him down behind the van. You guys let Juan Sr. go," Javier said.

"We will do our part. You and your damn parade behind you need to kill your headlights," Smooth ordered.

"Tell them to kill the lights," Javier ordered Tito, who exited the SUV with his M-16 rifle and walked back to his brothers.

Javier stared in the rear-view mirror until he saw all the lights go out and Tito return with two of his brothers.

"Okay, man. We're about to move first," Javier said to Smooth, who was still on the phone.

"Let's go then," Smooth replied.

Javier and Tito's two M-13 brothers grabbed Choppa from the backseat. He had passed out again, so the two men carried him by his hands and feet to the back of the van. They laid him down on the ground on his side. They then quickly ran back to the SUV.

"Your turn now," Javier said to Smooth.

"Send him out!" Smooth ordered his men.

No less than a minute had gone by when Javier saw the old man walking from the side of the van. Just about the same time, Smooth's men made it to Choppa.

"Damn, homie! Go grab the old man," Javier said to Tito, trying to make sure Juan Sr. was secured.

When Tito made a dash toward the old man, two shots pierced through his chest, dropping him.

All hell broke loose!

"They beat 'em!" Jay screamed as he released a deadly fusillade at Javier's SUV.

The Mexicans in the other SUVs were firing at the building where the shots were coming from and knocking them down.

Damn, I thought it was only three of them! Javier thought as he turned on his brights, ducked with his M-16, and climbed out of the passenger side door

The moment Javier's feet touched the ground, the old man was riddled with a storm of bullets.

"Nooo! Shit!" Javier screamed as he released a stream of bullets back at the building and the van he was leaving.

As he continued to shoot at the tail lights, he glanced at Tito, who was still moving.

"Hold 'em off!" Javier shouted as he continued to shoot into the dark confines of the building.

When he looked around, most of his men were down except a few.

Damn man! Javier thought.

A minute later, the shooting from the gym ceased, and Javier was left with ringing ears. But he could still hear the burning tires on the other side of the building.

"Damn it! We played right into their hands!" Javier shouted as he ran over to Tito, who was still breathing with a bloody smile.

"M-13 *vida por vida*," Tito said in pain.

"No, homie. Don't go on me," Javier begged Tito.

When Javier went to pick him up, Tito took his last breath.

"Damn it! It's not supposed to be you!" Javier shouted,

The other M-13 brothers went to check on the old man. Everyone knew who Juan Sr. was. However, when they turned him over onto his back, it was not him. It was just some random old Mexican man.

"*No es señior* Juan Sr.*"

When Javier heard what his brother said, he stood up and walked over to see for himself. When he looked down at the dead man who wasn't Juan Sr., he shrilled loudly. "Fuck!"

Javier was highly upset, and he wanted the blood of Smooth to spill from his mouth after he drank it. Smooth had created a monster, and Javier had every means of making him pay for the loss of his M-13 brother and friend, Tito.

* * *

Mall couldn't believe how badly they had beaten up Choppa. After leaving the gym, Smooth floored the pedal to Jackson Memorial Hospital and helped carry Choppa through the emergency room doors. The nurses and doctors put Choppa on a gurney and immediately rushed him to the ER.

"We found him like this behind a building. Help him!" Mall begged as he left the hospital with Smooth, Sue Rabbit, and Guru to avoid the authorities.

The entire ride over to the trap was quiet. All that ran through everyone's mind was retaliation. As Smooth pulled up to the trap house, he called Spencer.

"Hello."

"How bad is he?" Smooth asked.

"No one can tell what a deer looks like when it's skinned," Spencer responded.

"Good, now please finish him and deliver him back to his little Mexican joint. Dump him at the building just in case the crime scene investigators are still out there."

"When do you want this done?"

"As soon as the sun comes up," Smooth ordered, and then disconnected the line.

Everyone looked in their own zones in front of them.

"At least we got him back. No matter what his condition is, it'll never be like what they're about to see!" Smooth announced.

19

*J*uan was not a happy camper. He couldn't believe that Smooth had gruesomely murdered his father and skinned him like he was some type of wild animal. Juan lost it and retaliated the moment breaking news discovered his father's body behind the building next to his Mexican jukebox club.

The feds were everywhere responding to shootings and pulling up to scenes to find wounded and injured young men and teens. Mothers were afraid to let their kids go outside because the shootings were occurring all over Miami. Juan had definitely sent for Smooth's head. Juan was at his low-key spot with Mario, who was consoling him for his loss.

"Bro, I have to get that Negro!" Juan said as he snorted a line of coke through a straw on the kitchen table.

Mario was lying back on the sofa with his hands behind his head listening to Juan vent for hours on end.

"Bro, we need to just go at this muthafucka! I know how we can handle it, but you got to be heartless."

"What the fuck do you mean? I have no soul for shit right now. Don't you see what's going on, huh?" Juan exploded.

"Then take the bitch, Tracy, and make her give her little bitch up, bro!" Mario exploded, jumping from the sofa and staring Juan in his eyes, face-to-face.

"That ho wants us to spare her bitch—their bitch!" Mario emphasized.

"Your father means more than what Tracy wishes you to do. She wants Smooth dead, but has everything to kill him," Mario explained.

"Let's wait until shit cools down right now. Our every move is being watched," Juan replied as he then sat back down at the table to snort another line.

* * *

"It's scary out there, China," Tracy said to her while she was chopping up chicken for the fryer.

"Yeah it is, and it don't have shit to do with us," China replied.

She knew exactly what was going on, and all she could think about was Smooth's safety. Her worrying about Smooth felt like a ticking time bomb ready to explode with the devastating news that Smooth might be killed. She had the urge to call him and check up on him, but she didn't want to let him know that she cared about him and was still in mad love with him.

"You're right, China. I hope someone takes a bullet and puts it right between Smooth's eyes 'cause he—"

Smack!

Before Tracy could finish her sentence, China slapped the shit out of her, acting off her emotions. The slap was so loud that everyone in the back kitchen froze in their tracks and looked at the perfect couple that was always so happy.

"Don't you sit here and wish death on him and act like we don't have nothing. He don't deserve how you just all day wishing this and that—and now death. You must be out of your mind thinking I can stand that shit! If you want me to get over him, then you're going about it the wrong way. Because I'll kill anyone who wants him dead!" China explained to Tracy, who was still in shock that China had put her hands on her.

"Since you still love a man who's dragged yo' ass out and don't even appreciate you, go be with that nigga, China, and leave me alone!" Tracy said as she stormed out of the kitchen and off the job, humiliated.

China didn't feel bad at all, and that gave her an eerie feeling. It made her realize that what she felt for Tracy was not nearly as strong as how she felt for Smooth. Since she left Smooth, she had been engrossed in contemplative thoughts, wondering if she made a mistake leaving Smooth.

"China, are you okay?" Jane asked, seeing that China had tears running down her face that she didn't even realize.

China wiped away her tears, looked at Jane, and then broke down crying hysterically into her arms. "I can't leave him!"

"It's going to be alright, China. It's okay. We're here!" Jane said while hugging her.

Tabby and Roxy rushed to China's side from the front of the kitchen and embraced her too. Neither needed words to fathom what was going on. Roxy knew her sister, and she knew when she was stressing about Smooth.

* * *

Smooth didn't have China to drive with him up north to re-up, so he brought Amanda along. She was a good driver and very entertaining. When Smooth wasn't asleep, he was up listening to her entire life. With all the chaos in the city, Smooth informed Sue Rabbit and Guru that he was leaving town to re-up.

Miranda took a burden off his hands and agreed to watch Zorro after she gave Smooth the keys to his new mansion. Miranda admitted to Smooth that she would miss him as a neighbor, but she understood that he wasn't safe, especially after seeing the bullet-riddled home.

While Smooth turned his head and looked Amanda up and down, he thought, *She's beautiful. Why can't I wife her?*

Kelly Rowland's "Motivation" was playing at a low volume, and Smooth could see that Amanda loved the hit.

"Why are you staring at me? You know that's rude!" Amanda asked as she briefly looked at Smooth and then back at the road.

"Tell me something," Smooth began as he leaned his seat up while turning down the radio.

"Hey, that's my shit!"

"I know. So tell me, what motivates you, huh?"

"What do you mean by that, Smooth? By the way, we're in New York. Where are we going?"

"Find the first hotel, baby," Smooth directed, "and then back to the question."

"A lot motivates me, Smooth. Getting up every morning to see a new day stare me in my face motivates me. And knowing that I could be anything I want motivates me," Amanda said as she turned off an exit.

"Why do you help me out, Amanda, when you could be better off somewhere else and with a more deserving man?" Smooth asked.

"Because the day I was going to give it all up, a handsome teen came to my doorstep and changed my mind. Then he fucked me good one day and fucked my head up, baby boy. Now I'm playing number two until he decides to accept me as number one," Amanda said as she pulled into the Hilton parking lot.

"So I fucked your head up, huh?" Smooth asked as Amanda parked.

"You did something no man in my past has done to me. I could get on a plane and leave any day, but I would be leaving something precious behind," Amanda confessed.

"What you're feeling is deep, huh?"

"No, it's too deep. I know you're stuck between a rock and a hard place. That's okay. I've been there, and you will make up your mind—one day. Come, let's get some rest," Amanda said as she grabbed her Coach purse and got out of the Range Rover.

Inside the room, Smooth didn't let Amanda take two steps before he grabbed her and kissed her deeply. He closed the door with his foot and backed Amanda up to the bed, where they collapsed into each other's passion. Smooth tore off her blouse, and she pulled his black T-shirt over his head.

Smooth slid out of his jeans and set his Glock .22 on the floor. As he took off his briefs, Amanda slid out of her skirt and spread her legs for Smooth to dive in. Smooth plunged his cock deep inside her phat wet pussy and made love to her slowly.

* * *

China came back to her and Smooth's apartment and grabbed some extra clothes that were left behind when she had packed her things the day before.

I can't do it without him, China thought as she looked around at the bullet-destroyed apartment.

It then dawned on her that Zorro was not in the apartment.

Maybe he's out walking Zorro, China thought.

She had no clue that Smooth had moved out of the apartment and hadn't had a chance to clear out his clothes yet. China stuffed her clothes into her duffel bag and then walked out of the sad-looking apartment. She got in her Mercedes and traveled north of Florida on her way to Ocala to go see her boo, Jenny. It was Labor Day weekend, so she would be able to visit her from Saturday to Monday, where she would be able to tell her all that was going on.

* * *

"People, we have a war going on outside this room. We can't continue to just sit and let this drug war take control of our city," DEA Agent Debra Jones addressed the fifty other agents in the room.

She was a black woman in her mid-forties with a flawless ebony complexion. She was known as the pit bull in a skirt throughout Miami, who had taken down some of the roughest drugs lords throughout her twenty years on the DEA force.

She was the head DEA lieutenant over the sweep that was being planned in a couple of days. She wanted Juan José, Mario Lopez, and Stone Bolt, on whom she had a pile of evidence to throw them away for a lifetime. She hadn't yet figured out the face of Juan Jose's enemy, but she was sure she was heading in the right direction by preparing to sweep the streets.

"My fellow agents, we will be moving in on these seventeen blocks like a damn hurricane," Jones said, gesturing with her hands and pointing toward a blackboard filled with home addresses and names. "We will take down these monsters," she said, pointing at José's, Lopez's, and Bolt's mug shots.

"Agent Jones, will this be a morning bust all the way to noon?" an agent asked from the back of the room.

"Yes sir, this will be an early morning raid that will carry on until noon. We should be wrapping up our last bust precisely at 1:00 p.m.," Agent Jones explained.

"Will we interrogate on-site or bring them back for a proper interrogation?" another agent asked.

"We will have warrants for everyone we arrest. So no one will be free to leave or be picked up for the hell of it. We will interrogate to find the enemy that's not on this board," Jones added.

"It answers my question, ma'am. Thank you."

"You're welcome, sir," Agent Jones said, nodding her head.

"People, get some rest and report at headquarters in the morning," Jones concluded, and then walked from the room.

* * *

"Yellow!"

"Yellow!" Banga said to Smooth when he returned his call.

"What's good, fam?" Smooth asked.

"Shit! Just trying to see what's good with you. There's so much chaos going on down the way. My mama called me and said please don't come down, not even to see her," Banga explained.

"Shit crazy, bro. I had to get away and duck off for a couple days."

"Yeah, out of town?" Banga asked.

"Yeah, out of state, nigga."

"You and China?"

"Naw, me and China done split!"

"Get the fuck out of here. I'm not going for that, nigga!" Banga exclaimed, not believing Smooth.

Shit, they were like Bonnie and Clyde. Who gonna believe that shit? Banga thought.

"Yeah, bro. It's for real. She started tripping on me. And peep this shit, fam. She left me for another bitch!" Smooth explained.

"You serious, nigga?"

"Serious as a heartbeat, my nigga!" Smooth replied.

"Man, y'all was too good, Smooth," Banga said.

"I know, and she left like it wasn't nothing!"

"Damn! That shit don't even sound real."

"It is, bro! But I'm chilling in the Empire State with number two. We been fucking up a storm," Smooth bragged.

"Yeah, damn, nigga, you don't waste no time, huh?"

"Shit, since when do I?" Smooth replied.

"China gonna kill you *and* number two. Don't expect her to not come back, bro. She's only gone for a day or two. She'll be back when she can't breathe. Because, nigga, y'all two are like H_2O. Y'all need each other, bro," Banga said.

"I hear you, but she really gone about the bitch, Tracy. I had to slap the hoe down."

"Why?" Banga asked.

"Because she was all in a nigga business. That hoe brainwashed my bitch."

"No, I think prison did," Banga suggested.

"Yeah."

"You ever thought what it would have been like with Rebecca in the picture?" Bang asked.

Hearing Rebecca's name caused Smooth to feel a little grief.

"Always, bro," Smooth said.

"Naw, bro. I'm talking about how China would have dealt with you giving her a kid before you could give China one."

"She wasn't upset when I told her," Smooth reflected on when he had told China about Rebecca's death.

"Don't mean she wasn't feeling some type of way, bro," Banga said. "Bro, listen. If it's not just you and China, there's gonna be conflict. She adopted a double life, bro, and it got between y'all. If she comes back, then she'll realize that that's where shit went wrong too," Banga said.

"You're right, fam. Thank you," Smooth said, appreciating Banga bringing light to the situation at hand.

He needed someone to talk to about him and China. It was a relief. He had left Amanda in the hotel room while he stepped outside for some fresh air and to return Banga's call. He loved China and saw it in her eyes that she loved him too and was unsure if she was making the right decision.

She'll be back, he thought.

"Bro, don't beat yourself up. I can hear your stress. Just give her time to get her thoughts in order, bro!" Banga said.

"I'ma do that, bro," Smooth said.

"Okay, now before I let you go—because I got my bitch waiting on me to wrap up this call—when will you be through? Please tell me soon."

"I'ma be up here until Sunday. So I'll be there Monday to drop off something."

"Good, good. Cause I need it."

"How much?"

"I need twenty," Banga replied.

"Okay, but listen. How 'bout we do business at Rimes's so I ain't gotta come into Booker Park, because I can't let Meka see me, bro. I can't afford the hassle," Smooth explained.

"We could do that. Just call me when you get up there, and I'll slide through, bro," Banga said.

"Alright, bro. That'll be good. I'll see you when I touch down," Smooth said before hanging up the phone.

Smooth so badly wanted to call China, but his pride was now in the way.

She'll be back, Smooth thought as he headed back up to his hotel room.

20

"Jenny Davis, you have a visit!" the CO announced over the PA system.

Jenny was at the card table playing spades, with Carlisha as her partner.

"There goes that visit you've been waiting on," Carlisha said.

"Yeah, who are you picking as a partner?" Jenny asked, not wanting Carlisha to be in any bitch's face.

"I guess I'll pick Nay-Nay," Carlisha said, looking around for the bad-ass Puerto Rican.

"Don't play with me, Carlisha," Jenny said, giving her an evil look. "You had to pick the baddest bitch in the dorm, huh?"

"Stop tripping and go get dressed for your visit," Carlisha said, calling over Nay-Nay to grab Jenny's hand.

"Nay-Nay! Come get my baby's hand!"

Jenny stood up from her seat and handed over her hand to Nay-Nay while still giving Carlisha an evil stare.

"Stop it, boo. I'm not worried about nobody but you, okay?" Carlisha said.

"Okay," Jenny replied before she strutted away to her cell to prepare for her visit.

Damn! I can't wait to see my baby! Jenny thought as she changed out of her shorts and sports bra, and put on her visitation clothes.

When Jenny walked into the visitation area, she found sitting at the table with an assortment of food and drinks.

"Hey, honey!" Jenny called as she hugged and kissed China, who kissed her back passionately.

"Okay, ladies. Your minute to kiss is over!" an officer said while breaking up their embrace.

China rolled her eyes at the correctional officer and then sat down with Jenny.

"That hoe just hating 'cause she ain't got no one to kiss her ugly ass," China said, causing Jenny to erupt into laughter.

"Girl, you is crazy! How are you?"

"Miserable," China replied.

"Why? What's going on?" Jenny asked, seeing the stress on China's face.

"I left Smooth the other day, and I think I made a mistake," China explained. "Then I ran Tracy off yesterday."

Damn! Jenny thought. "Wow!"

"Yeah, right!" China agreed.

"How did all this happen?"

"He came home late the other night smelling like another woman. I went to pack my shit and told Tracy to come with me. She tried interrupting our argument."

"And Smooth slapped the shit out of her!" Jenny filled in the sentence.

"Yeah! How'd you know?" China asked, surprised.

"Because I would have slapped her ass too if she got in the way of a long-term relationship."

"Anyways, I ended up slapping the hell out of her because all day she was ranting on about Smooth, which I could understand. But when she wished death on him, I slapped the shit out of her!"

"Damn!" Jenny replied.

"Y'all just slapping Ms. Tracy all over the place."

"You just agreed she deserved it," China reminded her.

"Yeah, she did," Jenny said as she began eating her chicken sandwich before it got cold.

Pop!

Jenny opened a can of Coke and took a sip.

"So, where's Smooth?"

"I don't know. Probably trying to pay for a $2.3 million mansion," China said.

"Damn, girl. Don't you think we all need to be in the mansion?"

"It's not that, baby. Smooth don't have no job or career to account for a $2.3 million home. The feds would come snooping as soon as we lay our heads on the pillows," China explained.

"You have a point. So it's over, huh?"

"I don't know, Jenny. I can't stop thinking about him. Then yesterday he tried giving me the biggest diamond I've ever seen, and I turned him down," China explained, with tears forming in the wells of her eyes.

Before they could fall, Jenny grabbed China's hand.

"Baby, please don't let the world beat you when you know you have a shining prize just waiting to be let out. I'm here, and I'm not going nowhere."

"I know, Jenny," China sobbed. "It's just, I miss him already. I picked her over him. He came home smelling like another woman, but I knew he was handling his business with his cook girl."

"Do you think they have something going on?" Jenny asked.

"I don't know," China said, wiping her eyes and face with a napkin. "I never asked."

"Then ask her, baby! Go to her place and ask her to be a woman about things," Jenny suggested.

"Why would I step to another bitch? I'm supposed to check his ass, Jenny."

"You still would want to know about her to kill your curiosity, baby," Jenny said.

She's right, China thought.

"Do you want him back, China?"

"I don't know, Jenny."

"What about Tracy?"

"I don't think the three of us would ever work again."

"Well, what's not for him is not for you, China. Y'all been together too long. Yeah, he's deep in the streets and is for his homeboys. When he's around, does he treat you like a queen?" Jenny asked.

"Yes, he does," China said.

"When y'all go places, does he treat you like a queen in public?" Jenny said. "Baby, I read a book by Trayvon D.

Jackson. That man spits the truth in his book *True Love Dies Once*. He explains how a man gone will always be a man in the streets but a king at home. A king doesn't move without his queen. Smooth came back with that diamond and proved that to you. He loves you, China, and you gotta see that. I read your letters, and I know that you're worried about his safety. He understands that, but you got to understand that there's nowhere safe in this world, baby. Let a man be a man, boo," Jenny explained.

"What's the name of that book again?" China asked.

"*True Love Dies Once* by Trayvon D. Jackson," Jenny replied.

"I love you, girl. You've helped me. I think I got to go get our man back, baby."

"Go get him, baby, and just stick it out with him. Tell him how you feel about him coming in late. I know you, China. I know you blew up on him as soon as he stepped through the front door," Jenny said.

"You know I did," China replied, causing Jenny to laugh.

"Come, we have to take some pictures," China said as they stood from the table.

Together, she and Jenny took ten pictures and then went outside to get some fresh air. They enjoyed the sun as they walked around the visitors' track holding hands. China felt better, and she realized that coming to see Jenny was what she really needed. She was someone to pour her heart out to, who would understand her and correctly guide her.

* * *

Smooth and Amanda were enjoying each other's company at Da Silvano Italian restaurant on 6th Avenue in New York. They were on the roof that overlooked the city, feasting on mushroom risotto, whole grilled fish, and linguine with clams while enjoying a bottle of Bartenura Moscato.

"This fish is delicious. What made you bring me here?" Amanda asked, wiping her mouth with a napkin.

"I wanted to make my baby happy tonight."

"Oh yeah," Amanda said as she fed Smooth some of her fish after seeing that he had smashed his.

"Why does yours have a special spice to it?" Smooth said as he savored the taste of the fish.

"Because mine has extra sauce."

"Hot sauce?" Smooth questioned as his mouth began to burn.

He grabbed his Moscato and downed the whole glass.

"It's not that hot, boy."

"Shit! Where the hell are your taste buds?" Smooth asked as he pulled on his tie, pretending to die, which caused her to erupt in laughter.

"Boy, you're silly!" Amanda exclaimed.

"We're in New York. Maybe I could land a script if the right people see me."

"You have the right people right in front of you, baby," Amanda said as she slid her foot between Smooth's legs and pressed down on his dick.

"You want to make our own movie right here?"

"No, Smooth. Let's behave," Amanda said, snatching her foot back and slipping it back in her high heel.

"I really appreciate you bringing me here with you to New York. It's really good to get out of the apartment once in a while," Amanda said seductively while twirling her straw in her glass.

"Maybe we could do this more often," Smooth suggested.

"It'd be nice, as long as I'm with you, baby."

Damn, she sounds like China. I miss her, Smooth thought.

Amanda could sense the hurt coming on. She was a victim of a first love gone bad herself, and it was hard for her to get over her ex back in high school, who she had been with since middle school.

"I know it's hard, Smooth. But like I told you, I have patience for you," Amanda said.

"Thank you," Smooth said before he grabbed her hand.

"Take this dance with me, baby," Smooth said as he stood up and walked Amanda to the dance floor, where Italian music was playing and a few older couples were slowly dancing.

"Do you know what you're doing, boy?"

"When I'm in bed, I know what I'm doing, right?" Smooth asked.

"Yes, you do, baby."

"So why would I go wrong now?"

"No reason, baby," Amanda replied as she slowly and softly kissed Smooth. "I can't get enough of you, baby."

"And I can't get enough of you either, beautiful," Smooth answered.

"After this dance, can we go back to the room for the rest of the night?"

"Of course we can, baby," Smooth said.

"I think I'd love a chocolate dessert."

"And I'll take the caramel," Smooth added, squeezing Amanda's ass.

* * *

"Are you coming back before one o'clock, baby?" Tina asked Ham, who was lacing on his shoes and getting ready to go out into the night to hustle and find somewhere to smoke his crack.

"Yeah, I'ma be back. If you're asleep, I'll wake you up for some of that good pussy, baby."

"We'll see when you get back, baby," she said as she kissed him deeply.

Ham laid her back on the bed and started sucking on her neck. Tina was in a silk gown and wanted Ham to make love to her.

"Give it to me before you leave, daddy!" Tina purred.

"I can't." Ham jumped up before he got himself trapped.

I need a hit before I go crazy! he thought as he put on his jacket and shoved his 9mm into the waist of his pants.

"You better be back before 1:00 a.m. or yo ass going in the dog house. I'm not playing!" Tina said as she covered up under the blanket and turned her back to Ham.

"Baby, don't act like that. I said I'll be back. Now lose the attitude," Ham said as he stormed out of the room and apartment altogether.

When Tina heard the door slam, she got out of bed and walked to the bathroom, went underneath the sink, and grabbed her pouch. She was sexually frustrated, so she took two hits from her crack pipe.

"That'll do me fine until he brings his ass back," Tina said.

* * *

When Ham walked out of his apartment, he immediately pulled out his crack-weed blunt and took three long drags. He was walking down Magnolia Avenue, when he saw the two bubble headlights.

Oh, shit, po-po! Ham thought as he tossed the blunt on the ground.

The police put on their lights and whipped in front of him. He tried to run through a yard, but he was taken down by the fastest police officer on the force, nicknamed "Running Man."

"Where do you think you're going, Hamilton?" Running Man asked Ham while pulling his arm back.

Three other officers jumped onto Ham's back and began punching him in the head. Running Man was the sergeant and had a gang of officers ready to take down people like Ham.

"Stop resisting, sir. Stop resisting!" all three officers screamed while punching Ham in the head.

"I'm not resisting, man!" Ham hollered. "Awww, shit, man! That's my wrist. I'm not resisting," Ham cried out in pain when Running Man bent it back.

Running Man cuffed him and then yanked Ham up from the ground and slammed him onto the back of the police car. More police pulled up to the scene to assist. Running Man frisked Ham and found the 9mm and two ounces of crack.

"Hamilton, you're still out on bond from the first possession. Now you're in illegal possession of a firearm and too much crack to be smoking. So who are you selling for?" Running Man asked. "You threw down a crack blunt. Damn, Hamilton! I never thought you'd get turned out," Running Man said to Ham.

"Sergeant, I think he knows who he's selling for," an officer said.

Fuck! I'm done! Ham thought.

"We'll find out when we get to the station. We always give everyone an opportunity to come clean and help themselves out," Running Man said to Ham as he placed him into the backseat of the Martin County squad car.

Damn, I can't believe I'm leaving Tina out here again. I should have never left so fast, and I should have made love to her. Then I wouldn't be in this shit! Man, I can't go to prison. Hell no! Ham thought while looking at all the officers standing in front of the police car talking with each other.

When Running Man got into the car, Ham thought of a way out.

"Hey, Running Man."

"What do you want, Hamilton? It's not looking good for you at all, so please tell me a new song."

"Man, I can't go to prison."

"Well that's not your decision. It's the judge who's going to give you thirty-five years for these charges tonight," Running Man said as he typed in Ham's charges on his laptop.

"Man, listen. I smoke that shit."

"Okay, we'll see how stupid that looks to a judge."

"You got the blunt to prove it," Ham said.

"What blunt?"

"The one I threw on the ground," Ham replied.

"We never found no blunt, Hamilton," Running Man said, with a smile on his face.

"Y'all bitches dirty. You know the judge would see that I smoke and give me a lesser sentence. That shit ain't right!" Ham screamed, and then began kicking the window.

Running Man hopped out of the front seat and opened the back door. He then shot Ham with his Taser gun on a high setting.

"I bet that calms his ass down," Running Man said as he laughed with his fellow officers.

Everything was a blur to Ham. He only saw one face, and it belonged to the only one who could help him regain his freedom: Smooth.

* * *

Banga and his bitch, Quinny, were having a good time at Club Sugar Daddy's in Martin County, which had just opened two months prior. Everyone on the Treasure Coast came to get their club on. The club didn't close until 6:00 a.m. Banga was wasted and ready to get Quinny home so he could fuck the shit out of her.

"Baby, you think it's time for us to go? You about to fall over," Quinny shouted over the Rich Homie Quan song crunking the club.

Banga looked at the time on his watch and saw that it was 2:48 a.m.

"Yeah, let's get out of here. Daddy's ready to put this good dick on you."

"Oh yeah. Well, let's go!" Quinny said as she slowly led Banga through the crowd the best she could without him falling on anyone.

"Damn, baby. You don't need to get fucked up like this no more," Quinny said to him, when they made it outside to the parking lot.

When they got to the car, Quinny helped Banga inside on the passenger side, fastened his seat belt, and then gave him a kiss on his lips. Neither one of them saw the threat approaching. When Quinny backed out to close the door, two shots pierced through the back of her head and sent blood and brains onto Banga and the car.

"What the fuck!"

When Banga looked up, he only saw a masked man with golds in this mouth.

"We told you to take that shit back to Miami, nigga!"

Before Banga could reach for his TEC-9 underneath the seat, he was hit with a storm of bullets to his torso and face. The assassin then fled from the club on foot. Banga was dead from the first shot to his face.

21

O n Monday afternoon, China left Lowell Correctional Institution, trying every couple of hours to reach Smooth. Jenny had encouraged her to call him and let him back into her life. She was eager and dying just to hear his voice. But he was sending her calls to voicemail.

Shit, what am I supposed to expect? China thought as she traveled I-95 south on her way back to Miami. She even tried calling Tracy, who was also sending her messages directly to voicemail.

"Fuck her!" China said.

She had her mind made up. She was definitely leaving Tracy and going to try to work things out with Smooth. She couldn't leave him for anyone in the world. Jenny had told her the truth: Tracy was only concerned about stealing her from Smooth. If she had any love for Smooth, then she wouldn't let China leave Smooth. Tracy's intentions became transparent when Jenny explained to her how Tracy's hatred had built up.

"She don't love Smooth, so she won't love you," Jenny explained to China during visitation.

China's heart was for Smooth, and she was heading back to town to let Tracy know face-to-face that they were done. She grabbed all her clothes and then waited for Smooth to return to their apartment. China picked up her iPhone again and dialed Smooth's number, once again to no avail. He didn't answer, and it sent her directly to voicemail.

Don't worry, baby. I know I fucked up. But I will fix it, baby. I promise, China thought as she put her Mercedes on cruise control.

She wanted Smooth to hold her and make love to her like never before.

"I love you, Smooth," China said as she turned the Beyoncé song up and thought about their future. She vowed to never let anyone get between them again.

* * *

Smooth saw China persistently calling him, but he ignored all her calls. After seeing Jefe for re-up, he was back on the road.

Now she wants to talk. Well not on my time, baby. I tried to talk before, and you turned me down, Smooth thought as he coasted along I-95 heading back to Martin County.

Amanda was asleep in the passenger seat after driving halfway.

Smooth had been trying Banga's phone to get him prepared so when he came to Martin they could quickly handle business. Smooth looked over at Amanda and caught her staring at him.

"I thought you were asleep," Smooth said.

"You thought right. I just had a dream about you."

"Tell me about it," Smooth inquired.

"We were standing at the altar, hand in hand, and you put a big diamond on my finger and made me number one," she explained.

"Do you believe in dreams?" Smooth asked.

"I believe in reality. Dreams are signs and sometimes misleading," Amanda said.

"Wow!"

"What?" Amanda asked.

"That was deep," Smooth said.

Amanda unfastened her seat belt and then ducked down and crawled over to Smooth. She unfastened his belt, unzipped his jeans, and then pulled out his cock. She stroked him slowly until he was fully erect, and then she took his cock into her mouth.

"Damn, baby!" Smooth moaned.

"This my dick?" Amanda asked.

Smooth looked down at her and then back at the road. He saw that she was sucking his cock while tears were falling from her eyes. "Is it mine?" Amanda asked again, stroking Smooth slowly.

"Yes, baby. It's yours!" he told her as he exploded.

Amanda let him shoot his load down her throat. She cleaned him up, zipped his jeans back up, and then got back into her seat and closed her eyes for another catnap. She had him, but his heart and mind were still on China.

Smooth's phone rang again. When he looked at the number again, he saw that it was a call from the Martin County Jail.

"Who the hell is this? Please don't tell me that Banga's locked up, man," Smooth said as he answered the call.

"This is a collect call from Ham, from the Martin County Jail."

"What the fuck Ham locked up for?" Smooth said while pressing zero before the automated voice directed him to do so.

"This call may be recorded and monitored. Thank you for using GTL."

"What's good, Ham?"

"Man, they got me, bro," Ham told him.

"I see that, nigga. Where's Banga at? Please don't tell me he's in there with you," Smooth exclaimed.

"Nah, he's waiting on you."

"Shit, we supposed to be at Rimes's, bro. I can't come through the hood."

"Meka?" Ham asked.

"You already know," Smooth said.

"Man, I been calling Banga, but he not picking up. What's up? You talk with him?" Smooth asked.

"Yeah, his phone's been acting crazy. He said he'll pull up in the next hour, bro. Same spot, right?"

"Yeah, Rimes," Smooth replied.

"Bro, I got a high-ass bond."

"How much?" Smooth asked.

"$1 million."

"Damn, Ham. What's up?"

"A gun and two onions," Ham replied. "I need you, bro. Banga's coming through halfway."

"I got you, bro. Just let me get back in my city. Say no more!" Smooth replied.

"You have sixty seconds left," the automated voice announced.

"Alright, bro. Bet that up. I really appreciate you," Ham said.

"No sweat."

"Thank you for using GTL," the automated voice said before the call disconnected.

22

"*H*ello?" Guru answered his phone after seeing that it was Landi calling from work.

"Baby, get out of the trap now! They're about to raid! Please, they're suiting up now!" Landi screamed into the phone.

"What?" Guru asked.

"Baby, they're 'bout to fucking sweep. Get out of the trap!" she warned again.

"Okay," Guru said as he hung up the phone.

"Shut the trap down, Sue! Shut it down! They're raiding!" Guru screamed to Sue Rabbit, who began moving fast and stashing drugs in a duffel bag.

"Call everyone!" Sue Rabbit said to Guru.

Landi had put Guru up on beat weeks ago, and it was now going down. Guru called Mall first.

"Hello."

"Man, they raiding, bro."

Boom! Boom!

"Get down on the ground now. Get the fuck down!"

Guru could hear the raid live taking down Mall and Money.

"DEA, down on the ground!"

"Shit! They getting Mall and them now."

"Let's go," Sue Rabbit said as he made a dash out the door with Guru.

They both got into their own cars and got away from the trap house and drove to their low-key spot that no one knew about, not even Smooth. Like preparing for a hurricane, they had been ready for the raid to occur any day now. Sue Rabbit called Smooth's phone again. This time he got him to answer. He'd been calling him all day, trying to see if he was alright.

"Hello," Smooth answered.

"Man, please tell me you low-key!" Sue Rabbit said.

"What's up, bro?"

"Man, they hitting like a blazing fire!"

"Who?" Smooth asked.

"DEA, bro!"

"Please don't tell me that, bro!" Smooth answered.

"Man, it's true!"

"Shit! Shut down!" Smooth said as he hung up the phone pissed as hell.

* * *

Big Mitch was in the living room watching ESPN when the front door came down.

"DEA! Get the fuck down on the ground!"

The DEA swarmed inside, swaying their guns left to right and dropping everyone in the trap house.

"Big Mitch, who's your boss, huh?" Agent Jones asked.

"Hoe, this big dick in my pants is the boss. What? You want to suck it, bitch!" he said to her.

On Big Mitch's block, Agent Jones and the DEA had arrested 50 men with warrants.

* * *

"DEA! Down on the ground!" the officers screamed as they ran into Juan's brothel, laying down the entire place.

Agent Jones was furious after kicking down Juan's door and finding the place empty. She became even more furious when she took down Mario Lopez's door and found it empty as well. She couldn't believe how her raid was failing by just two men. She had swept all their blocks and arrested 97 Mexicans with warrants. The brothel had brought her count to 150.

I can't believe I missed these motherfuckers. How Lord? How? Agent Jones thought.

She had one more raid to do, and she would be interrogating all night. After seeing the brothel secured, Agent Jones and six of her men left to go pick up their last suspect.

* * *

Tracy was in her bedroom crying her eyes out because she was hurt by China, when she heard the knocks on the door. She didn't want to deal with anyone and had been ignoring China's call.

"Who the hell is it?" she said to herself.

She wanted to ignore the person, but they were knocking like a mad man.

She got out of bed and walked to the door. When she looked through the peephole, the person on the other side was blocking her sight with their finger.

There's only one person who would do that, Tracy thought as she opened the door.

"What, China?"

Tracy stopped short when she saw that the visitor was not China. The look on her face revealed trouble. It was too late for her to turn back and run like she wanted to, so she played it calm.

"Juan, why didn't you call me before you stopped?"

Before Tracy could get out her next word, Juan grabbed her around her throat and throttled her into unconsciousness. When she hit the floor, he stepped over her body and closed the front door. He then grabbed her by her hair and dragged her to the bedroom.

* * *

Stone was sitting in his living room watching the Jamaican soccer team take on America, when his front door came down.

"What the fuck!"

"DEA! Get down on the ground now!" Agent Jones shouted as she came in with her gun aimed at Stone.

Damn, mon! Stone thought as he got down on the ground with his hands on his head.

"Mr. Stone Bolt, you're under arrest. I swear, you better start thinking about talking and telling us where your boss is, b or you'll be sleeping in a federal bed for a lifetime," Jones threatened as she cuffed him and brought him to his feet.

Stone said nothing. He knew the procedure. If she was fishing, then they had nothing on him. Stone just looked at Agent Jones and smiled at her with an evil smirk on his face.

"We'll see how funny shit is when we send you away for life, fucker!" Agent Jones said as she escorted Stone to the back of her unmarked car.

All of Stone's workers had been arrested, and seven of his trap houses had been raided. Stone couldn't believe what was going on. But he wasn't the least surprised. He just prayed for a way out.

23

Smooth arrived in Martin and pulled up to the Rimes food market, parked, and then waited for Banga to show his face. China again was trying to get in contact with him, but he remained adamant and sent her to voicemail.

"Baby, I'ma go use the restroom. Do you want anything out of the store?" Amanda asked.

"Yeah, bring me some Doritos and a Coke."

"Okay, baby," she said as she stepped out of his Range Rover in a lustrous skin-tight minidress. Her big ass had everyone turning their heads.

Smooth heard his phone alert him of an incoming text. When he looked, he saw that it was from China. He opened the text and read the message: "You can ignore me all you want. Shit, you have a right to. I'm sorry, and I want my man back. I love you, and I'm worried about you. Please pick up the phone!"

Smooth smiled when he finished reading the text.

"I knew you'd get your mind right sooner or later," Smooth said as he raised his head up to look for Amanda. "What the fuck!" he exclaimed when he saw the parking lot swarming with Martin County DEA agents.

When Smooth tried to start the engine, his driver-side window was smashed. A muscular DEA agent pulled him from his SUV and slammed him to the pavement, knocking all the wind out of him.

"Down, fucker! Get down! Stop resisting!" the agent shrilled as they were on Smooth's back.

"Wrong county, homeboy!" Sergeant Running Man said as his agents brought Smooth to his feet and rushed him to an unmarked Yukon.

Smooth never saw Ham—whose job it was to point out Smooth to the agents—in the other unmarked car.

"Good job, Hamilton," Running Man said to Ham as they pulled away from the scene.

* * *

When Amanda saw the raid and that Smooth had been taken down, she walked out of the store and walked in the opposite direction.

"I can't believe this!" Amanda cried as she got far away from the scene.

She walked to McDonald's and called for a taxi to take her to Palm Beach, where she would catch another taxi to Miami. Amanda was hurt and felt empty without Smooth.

How did they know he was coming? Somebody set my baby up, Amanda thought as her taxi pulled up to her.

"Are you waiting for a taxi, ma'am?"

Amanda dried her eyes, and then walked toward the taxi and hopped into the backseat.

"Palm Beach, Florida, please."

"Yes, ma'am," the driver acknowledged.

* * *

For hours, Juan had been fucking Tracy in her asshole with no mercy. She was tied at her wrists, and her feet were bent over the bed.

"So you don't want to give the stankin' bitch up, huh?"

"Juan, please!" Tracy cried out as he continued to penetrate her asshole while holding on to her wrists.

"Juan! Okay, I will tell you!" Tracy cried out, yielding to Juan's sexual punishment.

Juan pulled out and wiped off his cock covered with blood and shit, with a wash rag.

"Why, Juan?" Tracy asked trembling. "I have been good to you. I told you that I would find out where Smooth stays. All I needed was time, Juan!" she cried.

"Bonita, time is running out. My father is dead, and you're fucking the enemy's bitch! I need your bitch!" Juan said, panting breathlessly while pulling off his belt.

"Where is she, bonita?"

"I don't know. We're . . . !"

Whack!

"Aww, Juan, please!" Tracy screamed out when Juan whipped her ass with a belt.

"Where is she, bonita?"

Whack!

"Please. No! No!"

"You lie to me, bonita!" Juan shouted.

Click! Click!

Juan froze when he heard the distinctive sound of a gun being cocked near his ear and pressed to the back of his head.

"Drop the belt wetback," China ordered, "and put your hands in the air."

Tracy was glad to hear China's voice. She knew that Juan would have killed her when he was done with her. Juan did what China commanded and put his hands up.

"So, you want my man so bad, huh? Well, you've found him, esé. Because we're one item, bitch!"

Bam!

China whacked Juan in the back of his head, causing him to fall unconscious onto the bed next to Tracy, who was still tied and bent over the bed.

"And bitch, you betraying-ass hoe! You were playing up under me to get my man killed!"

"Baby, I'm sorry. He made me. I swear," Tracy cried.

"Yeah, I know. But he ain't make you hate him. I thought you were beautiful, but you ain't nothing but a cold bitch!" China said as she aimed at Tracy's head. "All for what? Bitch!"

Boom! Boom! Boom! Boom!

China pulled the trigger, hitting Juan in his face and chest when he tried to charge her. He was dead when the first shot pierced through his eye. Tracy began crying when she saw Juan's body sprawled out on the bed, staining her sheets with blood and brain matter that flew onto her face.

"I heard everything, bitch," China said. "It's fucked up how you played me just to try and kill my nigga."

"I love you, China," Tracy cried.

"No, you didn't, bitch! If you loved me, then you would have loved Smooth," China said as she aimed the gun at

Tracy's head and pulled the trigger until her Glock was empty.

China grabbed everything that belonged to her and then left the chilling scene unnoticed.

Epilogue

Two months later

She was nervous as hell as she sat on the doctor's bed awaiting his return with her results.

Damn, what's taking him so long? she thought, with a stomach full of butterflies.

The symptoms were evident. She just needed the truth now. When she heard the voices outside the door, she strained her ears to try to catch any hint of her speculations and coming fate.

The door opened, and the doctor stepped in. He was an Arab who wore an excessive amount of cologne.

"Okay, ma'am. We have your results, and, ma'am, your tests came back positive."

"Oh my gosh! Oh my gosh!" She broke down crying hysterically.

To be continued . . .

BOOKS BY GOOD2GO AUTHORS

GOOD 2 GO FILMS PRESENTS

**THE HAND I WAS DEALT- FREE WEB SERIES
NOW AVAILABLE ON YOUTUBE!
YOUTUBE.COM/SILKWHITE212**

SEASON TWO NOW AVAILABLE

To order books, please fill out the order form below:

To order films please go to *www.good2gofilms.com*

Name:_____

Address:_____

City: _____ State: _____ Zip Code: _____

Phone:_____

Email:_____

Method of Payment: Check   VISA   MASTERCARD

Credit Card#:_____

Name as it appears on card: _____

Signature: _____

Item Name	Price	Qty	Amount
48 Hours to Die – Silk White	$14.99		
A Hustler's Dream - Ernest Morris	$14.99		
A Hustler's Dream 2 - Ernest Morris	$14.99		
Business Is Business – Silk White	$14.99		
Business Is Business 2 – Silk White	$14.99		
Business Is Business 3 – Silk White	$14.99		
Childhood Sweethearts – Jacob Spears	$14.99		
Childhood Sweethearts 2 – Jacob Spears	$14.99		
Childhood Sweethearts 3 - Jacob Spears	$14.99		
Childhood Sweethearts 4 - Jacob Spears	$14.99		
Flipping Numbers – Ernest Morris	$14.99		
Flipping Numbers 2 – Ernest Morris	$14.99		
He Loves Me, He Loves You Not - Mychea	$14.99		
He Loves Me, He Loves You Not 2 - Mychea	$14.99		
He Loves Me, He Loves You Not 3 - Mychea	$14.99		
He Loves Me, He Loves You Not 4 – Mychea	$14.99		
He Loves Me, He Loves You Not 5 – Mychea	$14.99		
Lord of My Land – Jay Morrison	$14.99		
Lost and Turned Out – Ernest Morris	$14.99		
Married To Da Streets – Silk White	$14.99		
M.E.R.C. - Make Every Rep Count Health and Fitness	$14.99		
My Besties – Asia Hill	$14.99		
My Besties 2 – Asia Hill	$14.99		
My Besties 3 – Asia Hill	$14.99		
My Besties 4 – Asia Hill	$14.99		
My Boyfriend's Wife - Mychea	$14.99		
My Boyfriend's Wife 2 – Mychea	$14.99		
Naughty Housewives – Ernest Morris	$14.99		
Naughty Housewives 2 – Ernest Morris	$14.99		
Naughty Housewives 3 – Ernest Morris	$14.99		

Never Be The Same – Silk White	$14.99		
Stranded – Silk White	$14.99		
Slumped – Jason Brent	$14.99		
Tears of a Hustler - Silk White	$14.99		
Tears of a Hustler 2 - Silk White	$14.99		
Tears of a Hustler 3 - Silk White	$14.99		
Tears of a Hustler 4- Silk White	$14.99		
Tears of a Hustler 5 – Silk White	$14.99		
Tears of a Hustler 6 – Silk White	$14.99		
The Panty Ripper - Reality Way	$14.99		
The Panty Ripper 3 – Reality Way	$14.99		
The Solution – Jay Morrison	$14.99		
The Teflon Queen – Silk White	$14.99		
The Teflon Queen 2 – Silk White	$14.99		
The Teflon Queen 3 – Silk White	$14.99		
The Teflon Queen 4 – Silk White	$14.99		
The Teflon Queen 5 – Silk White	$14.99		
The Teflon Queen 6 - Silk White	$14.99		
The Vacation – Silk White	$14.99		
Tied To A Boss - J.L. Rose	$14.99		
Tied To A Boss 2 - J.L. Rose	$14.99		
Tied To A Boss 3 - J.L. Rose	$14.99		
Time Is Money - Silk White	$14.99		
Two Mask One Heart – Jacob Spears and Trayvon Jackson	$14.99		
Two Mask One Heart 2 – Jacob Spears and Trayvon Jackson	$14.99		
Two Mask One Heart 3 – Jacob Spears and Trayvon Jackson	$14.99		
Young Goonz – Reality Way	$14.99		
Young Legend – J.L. Rose	$14.99		
Subtotal:			
Tax:			
Shipping (Free) U.S. Media Mail:			
Total:			

Make Checks Payable To:
Good2Go Publishing
7311 W Glass Lane,
Laveen, AZ 85339

CPSIA information can be obtained
at www.ICGtesting.com
Printed in the USA
LVOW04s1439100117

520453LV00010B/730/P